THE LITTLE WORLD
OF DON CAMILLO

THE
LITTLE WORLD
OF
DON CAMILLO

by

GIOVANNI GUARESCHI

Translated from the Italian by

UNA VINCENZO TROUBRIDGE

THE REPRINT SOCIETY LONDON

FIRST PUBLISHED 1951
THIS EDITION PUBLISHED BY THE REPRINT SOCIETY LTD.
BY ARRANGEMENT WITH MESSRS. VICTOR GOLLANCZ LTD.
1953

PRINTED IN GREAT BRITAIN BY RICHARD CLAY AND COMPANY, LTD.
BUNGAY, SUFFOLK

CONTENTS

The Little World

(Here, with three stories, is explained the world of the "Little World".)

WHEN I was a young man I worked as a reporter on a newspaper, and all day long I cycled about in search of stories worth reporting.

Then one day I met a girl, and I spent the daytime thinking about what she would do if I became Emperor of Mexico or if I should die. And in the evenings I would write up my column of news items invented by me, which people liked, as they were far more probable than true news items.

My vocabulary consisted of about two hundred words, and these were used to tell the story of the old man knocked down by a cyclist or the housewife who cut off the end of her finger while peeling potatoes.

So you must expect no real literature or anything

like that: in this book I am that same reporter, and I confine myself simply to relating items of news.

These are invented, naturally, and therefore very life-like, for dozens of times I have seen a story I have written, a couple of months later actually take place. There is nothing extraordinary about this— it's simply a question of reasoning: you take into consideration the time, the season, the customs and the psychological moment, and you can conclude that in a given set of circumstances such and such a thing will happen.

These stories, therefore, take place in a particular atmosphere and a particular place. The atmosphere is that of Italian politics from December 1946 to December 1947—the story, in fact, of one political year.

The place is a part of the Po Valley: and here I must point out that for me the Po begins at Piacenza. The fact that from Piacenza onwards it is still the same river is of no consequence: the section of the Via Emilia from Piacenza to Milan is still the same road, but the real Via Emilia goes from Piacenza to Rimini.

But you cannot compare a river with a road, because roads belong to history and rivers to geo-graphy.

And so?

Men do not make history: they endure it as they endure geography. And history, anyhow, is all a matter of geography.

Men try to change geography. They bore through mountains and change the course of rivers, and in so doing imagine they change history; but they change absolutely nothing because, sooner or later, everything will go to rack and ruin. Water will engulf their bridges, destroy their dams and fill their mines; everything will collapse, from the most miserable dwellings to the grandest palaces, and then grass will grow on the ruins and all will once again be earth. The survivors will find themselves with stones as their only weapons against animals, and history will repeat itself.

And it will be the same old history.

Then, three thousand years later, someone will find, buried deep in the mud, a drinking-water tap and perhaps a lathe made by Breda at Sesto San Giovanni,* and in amazement will exclaim: "Just look at this!"

* An industrial suburb of Milan.

And they will set to work to achieve the same stupidities as their ancestors. Because men are hopelessly condemned to follow progress, which leads irrevocably to a substitution of the Almighty of olden times by the newest chemical formulæ. And so, in the end, the Almighty is wearied, moves the tip of the little finger of His left hand a fraction of an inch, and the world is blown sky-high.

So the Po begins at Piacenza, which is a good thing, because it is the only worthwhile river in Italy: and the rivers one respects develop in the plains, because water is intended to remain horizontal, and only when it is quite horizontal does it possess all its natural dignity. The Niagara Falls are a rather vulgar fair-ground sight, like a man walking on his hands.

The Po begins at Piacenza, and at Piacenza begins the *Little World* of my stories, and this *Little World* lies in that stretch of plain between the Po and the Apennines.

But this is its atmosphere and this is its setting: and in a region like this, if you stop on the road and look at a farm house set in the midst of maize and hemp—immediately a story is born.

First Story

I LIVED in Boscaccio, in the Valley, with my father, my mother and my eleven brothers: I was the eldest, not quite twelve years old, and Chico the youngest, barely two. Every morning my mother handed me a basket filled with bread and some apples, or sweet chestnuts, and then my father would line us up in the yard and make us say out loud the Lord's Prayer; then we set off where our fancy took us, and did not return home till sunset.

Our fields were limitless, and we could have roamed all day long without going beyond our boundaries. My father would not have complained even if we had trampled on three whole fields of springing corn or uprooted a whole row of grapevines. Yet we always went beyond our own lands and got up to endless mischief. Even Chico, who was barely two years old and looked like a cherub, with his little red mouth and large, long-lashed eyes and curls over his forehead, was the last to let a gosling get away if it came within his reach.

Then, each morning, as soon as we had gone, old women would come flocking to the farm with baskets laden with dead goslings, hens and chicks, and my mother, for every dead bird, had to give a live one in exchange.

We had at least a thousand chickens scrabbling round in the fields, but if we needed a fowl for the pot it had to be bought.

My mother shook her head and went on giving live goslings for dead ones. My father scowled, twirled his long moustache and sternly cross-examined the women as to which of his twelve children had done the mischief. When one of the women told him it was Chico, the smallest, he had the story repeated three or four times; he wanted to know how he had managed to throw the stone, how big the stone was, and if he had hit the gosling with the first shot.

I learned about this some time later: in those days we did not think about it. I remember once, when Chico hurled a stone at a gosling which was foolishly waddling about in the middle of a bare field, and I was with the other ten watching from behind a bush, I saw my father about twenty feet away smoking his pipe beneath a large oak-tree.

When Chico had dispatched the gosling, my father walked quietly away, his hands in his pockets, and we all thanked the good Lord.

"He didn't notice a thing," I whispered to the others. But, then, I had no idea that my father had shadowed us all the morning, concealing himself like a thief, just to see how Chico killed goslings.

But I am digressing from the point, which is a common fault of writers with too many memories.

I must tell you that Boscaccio was a place where no one ever died, because of the wonderful air.

So to the people of Boscaccio it seemed incredible that a child of two should fall ill.

However, Chico became seriously ill. As we were returning home one evening he suddenly lay down on the ground and began to cry. Then he stopped crying and fell asleep. He would not wake up, so I lifted him. He was terribly hot and seemed full of fire: we were panic-stricken. The sun was setting and the sky was red and black and the shadows long. We left Chico where he was on the grass and ran away yelling and crying as if some terrifying monster were chasing us.

"Chico's asleep and he's boiling hot! . . . Chico's head is full of fire!" I sobbed as soon as I saw my father.

My father, I remember well, took his gun down from the wall, loaded it, tucked it under his arm and followed us without a word; we crowded round, no longer afraid, because our father was a man who could hit a hare eighty yards away.

Chico lay abandoned in the dark grass, and in his white clothes and with his curls on his forehead he looked just like a little angel of God who had broken one of his wings and fallen down into the clover.

As I said before, no one ever died in Boscaccio, and when the people heard that Chico was ill, they all felt a dreadful anguish. Even inside their homes they spoke in whispers. A dangerous stranger was wandering around the village, and at night no one dared to open their windows, for fear of seeing in their yard, white with moonlight, the black-robed hag, scythe in hand.

My father sent a carriage to fetch three or four famous doctors, who all felt Chico and put their ear to his back, then looked at my father in silence.

Chico continued to sleep and to burn, and his face was whiter than the sheets. My mother wept in the midst of us and would touch no food, while my father would not sit down and constantly twirled his moustache, not saying a word.

On the fourth day the three last doctors who had arrived together shrugged their shoulders and said to my father:

"Only the good Lord can save your child."

I remember it was morning: my father nodded to us, and we followed him into the courtyard. Then with a whistle he called in all the tenants, of whom there were fifty altogether, including men, women and children.

My father was tall, lean and powerful, with a long moustache, and he wore a large hat, a short, close-fitting jacket, his trousers tight over the thighs and long boots. (When he was young my father had been in America, and he liked to dress in the American manner.) When he stood, feet apart, towering over someone he looked quite frightening. He stood now, feet apart, in front of all his tenants and said:

"Only the good Lord can save Chico. Down on your knees: we must pray God to save him."

We all knelt down and began to pray aloud to God. The women said prayers in turn, and we and the men answered: "Amen."

My father remained stock still before us, arms akimbo, till seven o'clock in the evening, and everyone prayed because they feared my father and because they loved Chico.

At seven, as the sun was beginning to set, a woman came out to fetch my father. I followed him. The three doctors sat pale round Chico's bed.

"He's getting worse," said the oldest. "He will not live till morning."

My father said nothing, but I felt his hand grip mine tightly.

We left the room: my father took his gun, loaded it, slung it across his shoulders, and picking up a large package which he passed to me, said:

"Come along."

We walked across the fields: the sun was hidden behind the farthest clump of trees. We climbed over the wall of a garden and knocked on a door.

The priest was at home alone, eating by the light of an oil-lamp. Without stopping to remove his hat, my father went in.

"Father," he said, "Chico is ill, and only the good Lord can save him. To-day, for twelve hours, sixty people have prayed to the Lord, but Chico is getting worse and will not live till morning."

The priest looked at my father, his eyes wide with horror.

"Father," he continued, "you alone can speak to God and tell Him how things are. Make Him understand that if Chico does not get well again I will blow this place sky-high. I've ten pounds of dynamite in this parcel, so not a single stone of this church will be left standing. Come along!"

The priest could say nothing: he walked away, followed by my father, entered the church and, joining his hands, knelt before the altar.

My father stood in the middle of the church, his gun under his arm, feet wide apart, planted there like a solid rock. A solitary candle burned on the altar, and the rest of the church was in darkness.

Towards midnight my father called me: "Go and see how Chico is and come straight back."

I flew across the fields, and when I reached the house my heart was in my mouth. Then I ran back —even faster.

My father still stood motionless, feet wide apart, his gun under his arm, while the priest muttered prayers slumped on the altar steps.

"Daddy," I cried, with my last ounce of breath, "Chico is better! The doctor says he's out of danger! A miracle has happened! Everyone's smil-ing and happy!"

The priest got up: he was sweating and his face was drawn.

"Good," my father said brusquely.

Then, as the priest watched open-mouthed, he drew out from his pocket a thousand-lire note (in those days a very considerable sum for a farmer) and put it in the poor box.

"I'm a man who pays well for favours," he said. "Good night."

My father never boasted of this affair, but in Boscaccio there are still to-day some godless folk who say that that time God was afraid.

This is the Valley, a place where people do not christen their children, and blaspheme—not to deny God, but to spite Him. And yet it is only twenty-four miles or so from town; but in this plain traced with dykes, where you cannot see over a hedge or round the bend, each mile is like ten: and the town belongs to another world.

I remember:

Second Story

SOMETIMES one saw some town types at Boscaccio, mostly mechanics or masons. They came to tighten up bolts on the steel bridge over the river, or do some cement-work on the walls of the irrigation canal locks.

They wore straw hats or cloth caps on the side of their heads, and sat outside Nita's bar and ordered beer, and steaks and spinach.

Boscaccio was a village where the people ate at home and only went to the inn to swear a bit, play bowls and drink wine in merry company.

"Wine, bacon-soup and eggs with onion," Nita would answer, putting her head round the door.

Then the men would shove their hats or their caps on the back of their heads and start making loud remarks about Nita's various charms, the while banging on the tables and making as much racket as in a barn-yard.

The townsfolk understood nothing: when they were in the country they behaved like sows in a maize-field: they made noise and trouble. They ate meat-balls at home, but when they came to Boscaccio they asked for beer, which they drank out of bowls, and tried to browbeat men like my father, who owned three hundred and fifty beasts, had twelve children and fifteen hundred acres of land.

Now things are different, because in the country, too, there are men who wear their caps at a rakish angle, eat meat-balls and call out after the girls in the inns about their nice this and that: wireless and the railway have had a lot to do with this. But in those days things were not like this, and when the town types came to Boscaccio there were some who debated whether to go out with their guns loaded with shot or bullets.

Boscaccio was like that.

One day we were sitting round the work-bench in the yard and watching our father with a pick making a corn spade from a piece of poplar, when Chico came running up.

"Uh! uh!" said Chico, who, being only two, couldn't make very long speeches. I cannot understand how my father could always interpret Chico's burblings.

"It seems there's a stranger or queer animal somewhere," said my father, and having one of us bring his gun, he walked off, led by Chico, towards the field in front of the first ash-tree.

There we found six wretches from town, who with a tripod and red-and-white striped poles were measuring goodness knows what, and calmly treading down our clover.

"What do you think you're doing?" my father asked the nearest, who was holding up one of the red-and-white poles.

"Doing my work," the idiot replied, without turning round, "and if you did yours we would save a lot of breath."

"Get out!" shouted the others who stood in the clover gathered round the tripod.

"Be off!" said my father, pointing his gun at the six fools from the town.

When they saw him, tall as a poplar, standing in the path, they gathered up their instruments and scurried off like rabbits.

In the evening, while we sat in the yard watching our father give the finishing touches to the spade he was making, the six townsmen came up, together with two policemen whom they had had to go as far as Gazzola station to dig up.

"That's the man," said one of the six wretches, pointing at my father.

My father went on working without even looking

up, and the senior policeman said he could not understand how such a thing could have happened.

"What happened is that I saw five strange people ruining my clover, so I sent them off my land," my father explained.

The sergeant said that the men were an engineer and his assistants who had come to take measurements in connection with the steam tram-track which was to be built.

"They should have said so. If anyone wants to come on to my land they must ask permission," declared my father, eyeing his work with satisfaction. "And besides, no tram will pass through my fields."

"If it suits us, it will," the engineer laughed angrily.

But my father had noticed that the spade had a lump on one side, and was now busy flattening it out.

The sergeant said that my father had to let the engineer and his assistants through.

"It's to do with the Government," he concluded.

"When I see a paper with Government stamps I shall let them through," my father muttered. "I know my rights!"

The sergeant agreed that my father was right, and that the engineer should bring a paper with an official stamp.

The engineer and his five assistants returned the next day: they came into the yard, straw hats tilted and berets over one ear.

"Here's the letter," said the engineer, handing my father a sheet of paper.

My father took it, and we followed him indoors.

"Read it slowly," my father said to me when we were in the kitchen.

I read it twice.

"Go and tell him he can go ahead," said my father darkly.

When I came back I followed my father and the others up into the loft, where we all gathered at the round window that looked right over the fields.

The six fools walked cheerfully along the cart-track as far as the first ash-tree. Suddenly we saw them gesticulating furiously. One of them made as if to run back to our house, but the others restrained him.

Townsfolk, even to-day, always do that: they make as if to go after someone, but the others hold them back.

They stood arguing for a while on the path, then they took off their shoes and socks and rolled up their trousers. Finally they went skipping into the clover-field.

It had been a devil of a job, from midnight to five in the morning: four heavy-duty ploughs drawn by eighty oxen had completely ploughed up the clover-field. Then we had to stop up some ditches and open others in order to flood the ploughed field. Finally, we brought ten tanks full of sewage from the stables and tipped it into the water.

My father stayed with us at the window until midday, and we watched the men skipping about.

Chico made little gurgling noises every time he saw one of the six nearly trip up, and my mother, who came up to tell us lunch was ready, was highly delighted.

"Look at him: he's got all his colour back since this morning. He really needed to let himself go a bit, poor thing! God be praised for giving you that wonderful idea last night," she said.

Towards evening the six came back with the police, and a man in black—collected from God knows where.

"These gentlemen say that you purposely flooded

a field to hinder their work," said the man in black, very annoyed because my father did not get up and would not even look at him.

My father gave his usual whistle, and the tenants, all fifty of them, men, women and children, came into the yard.

"These people say that last night I flooded the field by the ash-tree," my father explained.

"It's over three weeks since that field was flooded," said one old man.

"Yes, over three weeks," they all said.

"They're confusing it with the clover-field next to the second ash-tree," said the cowman. "It's easy to confuse them if you're not familiar with these things."

So they all went away, fuming with rage.

The next morning my father had the horse harnessed to the trap and set off for town, where he stayed three days. He came back looking very glum.

"The track must pass there, there's nothing to be done," he explained to my mother.

Other men from the town came who began to stick wooden stakes between the now dry lumps of earth: the track, apparently, had to cross our clover-field, then rejoin the road and follow it as far as Gazzola station.

The steam tram would come from the town right to Gazzalo station, and would have been very useful: but it would have to go right across my father's land. And it would be crossing by means of force—that was the serious part. If they had asked my father politely, he would have been quite agreeable and given up the land without even asking for payment—for my father was not against progress. After all, was not he the first man to have a modern gun with an inside firing-pin?

But like this, good heavens!

Long lines of men from town came to work along the main road. They laid stones, put down sleepers and bolted down rails; and as the track gradually lengthened, the engine, which towed wagon-loads of materials, advanced. At night the workmen slept in open wagons at the end of the convoy.

Now the line was approaching the clover-field, and one morning the men began cutting down part of the hedge. My father and I were sitting under the first ash-tree, and with us was Gringo, our mongrel, whom my father loved as if he were one of us. Hardly had their spades cut the hedge when Gringo bounded towards the road, and when the men had made themselves a way through they came upon him snarling threateningly.

One idiot stepped forward, and Gringo went for his throat.

There were thirty of them with their picks and shovels: they could not see us because we were behind the ash-tree.

The engineer advanced brandishing a stick.

"Get away, you brute," he shouted.

But Gringo dug his teeth into his leg, and he fell to the ground with a yell.

The rest attacked in a mass, aiming blows at Gringo with their spades. But Gringo would not give in. He was bleeding, but he went on biting, tearing calves and crunching hands.

My father sat chewing his moustache: he was as white as a sheet and sweating. If he had whistled, Gringo would have come away immediately, and his life would have been saved. But my father did not whistle: he went on watching, pale as death, the sweat standing out on his brow, and gripping my hand while I sobbed.

My father's gun leant against the trunk of the ash-tree, and there it stayed.

Now Gringo's strength was failing and he struggled on only with his spirit. One of the men struck him on the head with the blade of his shovel and another pinned him to the ground with his spade. Gringo moaned a bit, then died.

Then my father got up, put his gun under his arm, and went slowly towards these men from the town. When they saw him appear before them, tall as a poplar, with his pointed whiskers, his wide brimmed hat, his short jacket and tight-legged trousers, they all took a step back and stared dumbly at him, gripping the handles of their tools.

My father went up to Gringo, bent down, took hold of his collar and dragged him away like a bundle of rags.

We buried him at the foot of the bank, and when I had trodden down the earth and smoothed it over, my father took off his hat.

I took mine off, too.

The tram never reached Gazzola. It was autumn, and the river was swollen and yellow with mud; one night the bank collapsed and the water ran over the fields and flooded all the lower part of the farm: the clover-field and the road became a small lake.

Then they stopped work altogether, and, so as to

avoid future dangers, ended the line at Boscaccio, about four miles from our house.

Then, when the river had subsided, my father, gripping me tightly by the hand, went with the men to repair the damage.

There we found the bank had broken just in the place where we had buried Gringo.

Such is the strength of a dog's soul.

I say that this is the miracle of the Valley.

This is the world of the Little World: long, straight roads, small houses painted red, yellow and ultramarine, tucked away between rows of vines. On summer evenings, behind the river bank, appears a large red moon that seems to belong to another age. Someone is sitting on a pile of gravel on the edge of the ditch, his bicycle leaning up against a telegraph pole. He's rolling himself a cigarette. As you pass he asks you for a match. You get talking. You tell him that you are going to the "festival" to dance, and he shakes his head. You tell him there are lots of pretty girls there, but he shakes his head again.

Third Story

GIRLS? No, no girls. For a bit of fun at the inn, or a sing-song, always ready. But nothing else: I have my girl already, and she waits for me every evening by the third telegraph pole along the Factory road.

I was fourteen, and as I cycled home one evening along the Factory road I noticed the branch of a plum-tree jutting out over a low wall, and stopped.

A girl with a basket in her hand came out, and I called to her. She must have been about nineteen, because she was much taller than me and well developed.

"Come and give me a leg up," I said.

The girl put her basket down, and I climbed up on to her shoulders.

The branch was overladen, and I filled my shirt till it was bulging with golden plums.

"Hold out your apron, and we'll go halves," I said to the girl.

She replied that there was no need.

"Don't you like plums?" I asked.

"Yes, but I can pick them whenever I like," she explained. "The tree is mine: I live here."

I was then fourteen and wore short trousers: but I was a bricklayer's lad and was afraid of no one. She was much taller than me and almost a full-grown woman.

"It's all very well to make fun of me," I said, scowling at her, "but I am quite capable of bashing your face in, you ugly old lamp-post."

She didn't say a word.

I saw her two evenings later on the same little road.

"Hi! lanky!" I shouted, then blew a raspberry at her. I couldn't do it now, but then I excelled my foreman at it, who had learnt how in Naples.

I saw her again several times, but didn't speak to her. Finally, one evening I lost my patience, jumped off my bicycle and blocked her way.

"Would you mind telling me why you're looking at me like that?" I asked, shoving the peak of my cap on one side.

The girl opened wide two eyes as clear as water. Never had I seen such eyes.

"I'm not looking at you," she replied timidly.

I got back on my bicycle.

"Watch your step, lanky," I shouted. "I'm a tough customer."

A week later I saw her in the distance in front of me walking along with a young man, and I was filled with rage. I stood up on the pedals and started cycling like mad. When I got within about two yards of the fellow I swerved, and as I passed him I gave him such a shove that he went sprawling on the ground.

I could hear him calling me a son of a bitch, so I got off my bicycle and leant it up against a telegraph pole, near a heap of gravel. He ran towards me in a fury. He was a young man of about twenty, and could have made mincemeat of me with one punch. But I was a bricklayer's lad and afraid of no one. At the right moment I threw a stone at him that caught him slap in the face.

My father was a first-rate mechanic, and when he had a spanner in his hand a whole village would turn tail and run. However, even my father, when he saw I had managed to pick up a stone, gave in and waited till I was asleep in order to hit me. My father, mark you! So imagine this silly fool! I had covered his face with blood; then in my own time I jumped on my bike and cycled off.

For a couple of evenings I gave the place a wide berth, then, on the third, I came back along the Factory road, and as soon as I saw the girl I cycled up to her and jumped off the saddle backwards, American style.

Boys on cycles to-day make me laugh: with their elaborate mudguards, bells, brakes, electric lamps, speed-gears and so on. I had a Frera which was a bit rusty, but to go down the sixteen steps to the square I never got off: I gripped the handle-bars like Gerbi and flew down like lightning.

When I came up to the girl, I took a small hammer out of my bicycle basket and held it up to her.

"If I find you with anyone else, I'll bash his head in, and yours," I said.

The girl looked at me with those accursed limpid eyes of hers.

"Why do you say that?" she murmured.

I didn't know, but does it matter?

"Because I say so," I replied. "You must either go out with me, or with no one."

"But I'm nineteen and you can't be more than fourteen," said the girl. "If you were eighteen it would be different. I'm now a woman, but you're a boy."

"Then you can wait till I'm eighteen," I shouted.

35

"And mind I don't see you with anyone else, or you'll be for it."

I was then a bricklayer's lad and was afraid of no one. When men started talking about women, I pushed off. I couldn't have cared less about them: still, I wasn't going to have this one playing around with others.

Every evening for four years I saw her, except on Sundays. There she always was, leaning against the third telegraph pole along the Factory road. If it was raining she had her umbrella up.

I never stopped once.

"Hello," I would say as I passed.

"Hello," she replied.

On my eighteenth birthday I stopped and got off my bicycle.

"I'm eighteen," I said. "Now you can come for a walk with me. And if you play the fool, I'll let you have it."

She was now twenty-three and a fully grown woman, yet her eyes were still as clear as water and she spoke softly, as before.

"You are eighteen," she replied, "but I'm twenty-three. The boys would throw stones at me if they saw me around with someone as young as you."

I let my bicycle fall to the ground, picked up a flat stone and said:

"You see that insulator there, the first one on the third pole?"

She nodded.

I hit it fair and square, and only the bare hook remained.

"Before boys start throwing stones at us," I declared, "they should learn to throw like that."

"It was just a manner of speaking," she said. "It looks bad for a woman to go around with a boy under twenty-one. If at least you had done your military service!"

I twisted my cap right round to the left.

"Listen, my good girl, what do you take me for? When I've been a soldier I'll be twenty-one and you'll be twenty-six, and then you'll start the same story all over again."

"No, I won't," the girl replied. "Between eighteen and twenty-three is one thing; between twenty-one and twenty-six quite another. The older one gets the less a difference in age matters. After all, there's very little to choose between a man of twenty-one and a man of twenty-six."

This seemed fairly reasonable to me: however, I wasn't the sort to be led up the garden-path.

"All right, we'll discuss the whole thing again when I've been a soldier," I said, jumping on my bike. "But, mind, if I don't find you when I get back, I'll bash your head in, even if I've got to come and drag you out from under your father's bed."

Every evening after that I saw her standing by the third telegraph pole, but I never stopped.

I said good-evening, and so did she.

When at last I was called up, I shouted to her:

"To-morrow I go into the army."

"Au revoir," she replied.

I'm not going to tell you now all about my life in the army: I sweated out eighteen months in the army, during which time I was just the same as when I was at home. I must have done three months' detention; and practically every evening I was either confined to barracks or in the cells.

As soon as the eighteen months were up I was sent home.

I arrived in the late afternoon, and without stopping to change into civvies, I jumped on my cycle and set off towards the Factory road.

If that girl had any more excuses, I'd do her in with my bicycle.

It was getting dark, and I sped along like lightning, wondering how on earth I was going to find her. But I didn't need to look far: there she was waiting for me by the third telegraph pole.

She was the same as when I had left her, and her eyes had not changed a bit.

I dismounted before her.

"I've finished," I said, showing her my discharge paper. "There's Italy sitting down, which means final discharge. When it shows Italy standing up, it means provisional discharge."

"That's good," said the girl.

I had raced like the wind, and my throat was dry.

"What about some of those yellow plums?" I asked.

The girl sighed:

"I'm so sorry, but the tree's burnt down."

"Burnt?" I exclaimed. "Since when do they burn plum-trees?"

"It was six months ago," the girl replied. "One night the hay-loft caught fire, and the house and all the trees in the orchard were burnt. Everything burned: after a couple of hours only the walls were left standing. Don't you see them?''

I looked over, and saw a bit of black wall with a window open to the red sky.

"And you?'' I asked.

"Me too,'' she murmured with a sigh. "A little heap of ashes and that's all.''

I looked at the girl leaning against the telegraph pole: I looked at her fixedly, and as I looked, through her face and her body I saw the grain of the wood of the pole and the grass of the ditch.

I put a finger on her forehead and touched the telegraph pole.

"Did I hurt you?'' I asked.

"Not at all.''

We stayed silent for a while, as the sky gradually turned a deeper red.

"So?'' I said finally.

"I waited for you,'' sighed the girl, "to show you it wasn't my fault. May I go now?''

I was then twenty-one, and could have presented arms with a cannon. When girls saw me pass they stuck out their chests as if on parade, and stared at me till their eyes nearly popped out.

"So?'' she repeated in a low voice. "May I go?''

"No," I replied. "You must wait until I've finished my life service. You're not getting away from me, my beauty."

"Very well," she said. And I fancied she smiled.

But these sort of things make me embarrassed, and I jumped quickly on to my bicycle.

We've now been seeing each other every evening for twelve years. I pass by without getting off my bike.

"Hello."

"Hello."

You see? If it's a matter of a sing-song at the inn or a bit of fun, always ready. But nothing else: I have my own girl who waits for me every evening by the third telegraph pole along the Factory road.

You may now ask: my friend, why do you tell me these stories?

Just because, I reply. Because I want you to realize that in that stretch of land between the river and the mountains things happen that could not happen anywhere else. These things fit in with the landscape. Here both the living and the dead breathe a wonderful air, and even the dogs have souls. If you remember this, you will all the better understand Don Camillo, Peppone and all the others. And you will not be surprised to hear Christ speak, or to read that a man can knock another over the head, fairly, of course, without hatred; and that in the end two enemies find they agree about essentials.

For the deep, eternal breath of the river freshens the air—this calm, majestic river along whose banks towards evening, Death passes swiftly by (on a bicycle!). Or you walk along the bank at night, stop to sit down and look down at a little graveyard that lies there below the bank. And if a spirit comes and sits beside you, you talk to it and are not afraid.

That is the kind of air one breathes in that far-away chunk of land, and so you can understand what can happen with politics there.

There is one more thing. In my stories Christ often speaks from His Cross. This is because He is one of my three principal characters: Don Camillo the parish priest, Peppone the Communist and Christ on the Cross.

Still a further word is needed: if any priest feels offended by my treatment of Don Camillo, he is quite welcome to break the biggest candle he can find over my head. And if any Communist feels insulted by my portrait of Peppone, he, too, is quite welcome to break a hammer and sickle on my back. But if anyone is offended by the conversations of Christ, there is nothing I can do about it: for the voice in my stories is not that of Christ, but of *my* Christ—that is, the voice of my conscience.

These are my own personal thoughts. . . .

So: every man for himself and God for all.

THE LITTLE WORLD
OF DON CAMILLO

A CONFESSION

DON CAMILLO had been born with a constitutional preference for calling a spade a spade. Upon a certain occasion when there had been a local scandal involving landowners of ripe age and young girls of his parish he had, in the course of his Mass, embarked upon a seemly and suitably generalized address, when he had suddenly become aware of the fact that one of the chief offenders was present among the foremost ranks of his congregation. Flinging all restraint to the four winds and also flinging a hastily snatched cloth over the head of the Crucified Lord above the high altar in order that the divine ears might not be offended, he had set his arms firmly akimbo

47

and had resumed his sermon. And so stentorian had been the voice that issued from the lips of the big man and so uncompromising had been his language that the very roof of the little church had seemed to tremble.

When the time of the elections drew near, Don Camillo had naturally been explicit in his allusions to the local leftists. Thus there came a fine evening when, as he was going home at dusk, an individual muffled in a cloak sprang out of a hedge as he passed by and, taking advantage of the fact that Don Camillo was handicapped by his bicycle and by a large parcel containing seventy eggs attached to its handle-bars, belaboured him with a heavy stick and promptly vanished as though the earth had swallowed him.

Don Camillo had kept his own counsel. Having arrived at the presbytery and deposited the eggs in safety, he had gone into the church to discuss the matter with the Lord, as was his invariable habit in moments of perplexity.

"What should I do?" Don Camillo had inquired.

"Anoint your back with a little oil beaten up in water and hold your tongue," the Lord had replied from above the altar. "We must forgive those who offend us. That is the rule."

"Very true, Lord," agreed Don Camillo, "but on this occasion we are discussing blows, not offences."

"And what do you mean by that? Surely you are not trying to tell Me that injuries done to the body are more painful than those aimed at the spirit?"

"I see Your point, Lord. But You should also bear in mind that in the beating of me, who am Your minister, an injury has been done to Yourself also. I am really more concerned on Your behalf than on my own."

"And was I not a greater minister of God than you are? And did I not forgive those who nailed Me to the Cross?"

"There is never any use in arguing with You!" Don Camillo had exclaimed. "You are always in the right. Your will be done. We must forgive. All the same, don't forget that if these ruffians, encouraged by my silence, should crack my skull, the responsibility will lie with You. I could cite several passages from the Old Testament. . . ."

"Don Camillo, are you proposing to instruct

Me in the Old Testament? As for this business, I assume full responsibility. Moreover, strictly between ourselves, the beating has done you no harm. It may teach you to let politics alone in My house."

Don Camillo had duly forgiven. But nevertheless one thing had stuck in his gullet like a fishbone: curiosity as to the identity of his assailant.

Time passed. Late one evening, while he sat in the confessional, Don Camillo discerned through the grille the countenance of the local leader of the extreme leftists, Peppone.

That Peppone should come to confession at all was a sensational event, and Don Camillo was proportionately gratified.

"God be with you, brother; with you who, more than any other man, have need of His holy blessing. It is a long time since you last went to confession?"

"Not since 1918," replied Peppone.

"You must have committed a great number of sins in the course of those twenty-eight years, with your head so crammed with crazy notions. . . ."

"A good few, undoubtedly," sighed Peppone.

"For example?"

"For example, two months ago I gave you a hiding."

"That was serious indeed," replied Don Camillo, "since in assaulting a minister of God, you have attacked God Himself."

"But I have repented," exclaimed Peppone. "And, moreover, it was not as God's minister that I beat you, but as my political adversary. In any case, I did it in a moment of weakness."

"Apart from this and from your membership of your accursed Party, have you any other grave sins on your conscience?"

Peppone spilled all the beans.

Taken as a whole, his offences were not very serious, and Don Camillo let him off with a score of Paters and Aves. Then, while Peppone was kneeling at the altar rails performing his penance, Don Camillo went and knelt before the crucifix.

"Lord," he said, "You must forgive me, but I am going to beat him up for You."

"You are going to do nothing of the kind," replied the Lord. "I have forgiven him, and you must forgive him also. All things considered, he is not a bad soul."

"Lord, you can never trust a Red! They live by lies. Only look at him; Barabbas incarnate!"

"It's as good a face as most, Don Camillo; it is your heart that is venomous!"

"Lord, if I have ever served You well, grant me just one small grace: let me at least break this candle on his shoulders. Dear Lord, what, after all, is a candle?"

"No," replied the Lord. "Your hands were made for blessing, not for striking."

Don Camillo sighed heavily.

He genuflected and left the sanctuary. As he turned to make a final sign of the Cross he found himself exactly behind Peppone, who, on his knees, was apparently absorbed in prayer.

"Lord," groaned Don Camillo, clasping his hands and gazing at the crucifix, "my hands were made for blessing, but not my feet!"

"There is something in that," replied the Lord from above the altar, "but all the same, Don Camillo, bear it in mind: only one!"

The kick landed like a thunderbolt and Peppone received it without so much as blinking an eye. Then he got to his feet and sighed with relief.

"I've been waiting for that for the last ten minutes," he remarked. "I feel better now."

"So do I!" exclaimed Don Camillo, whose heart was as light and serene as a May morning.

The Lord said nothing at all, but it was easy enough to see that He, too, was pleased.

A BAPTISM

ONE DAY the church was unexpectedly invaded by a man and two women, one of
whom was Peppone's wife.

Don Camillo, who from the top of a pair of steps
was cleaning St. Joseph's halo with Brasso, turned
round and inquired what they wanted.

"There is something here that needs to be baptized," replied the man, and one of the women held
up a bundle containing a baby.

"Whose is it?" inquired Don Camillo, coming
down from his steps.

"Mine," replied Peppone's wife.

"And your husband's?" persisted Don Camillo.

"Well, naturally! Who else do you suppose

gave it to me?" retorted Peppone's wife indignantly.

"No need to be offended," observed Don Camillo on his way to the sacristy. "Haven't I been told often enough that your Party approves of free love?"

As he passed before the high altar Don Camillo knelt down and permitted himself a discreet wink in the direction of the Lord. "Did You hear that one?" he murmured with a joyful grin. "One in the eye for the godless ones!"

"Don't talk rubbish, Don Camillo," replied the Lord irritably. "If they had no God, why should they come here to get their child baptized? If Peppone's wife had boxed your ears it would only have served you right."

"If Peppone's wife had boxed my ears I should have taken the three of them by the scruff of their necks and . . ."

"And what?" inquired the Lord severely.

"Oh, nothing; just a figure of speech," Don Camillo hastened to assure Him, rising to his feet.

"Don Camillo, watch your step," said the Lord sternly.

Duly vested, Don Camillo approached the font.

"What do you wish to name this child?" he asked Peppone's wife.

"Lenin Libero Antonio," she replied.

"Then go and get him baptized in Russia," said Don Camillo calmly, replacing the cover on the font.

The priest's hands were as large as shovels, and the three left the church without protest. But as Don Camillo was attempting to slip into the sacristy he was arrested by the voice of the Lord.

"Don Camillo, you have done a very wicked thing. Go at once and bring those people back and baptize their child."

"But, Lord," protested Don Camillo, "You really must bear in mind that baptism is not a jest. Baptism is a very sacred matter. Baptism is . . ."

"Don Camillo," the Lord interrupted him, "are you attempting to teach Me the nature of baptism? Did I not invent it? I tell you that you have been guilty of gross presumption, because, suppose that child were to die at this moment, it would be your fault if it failed to attain Paradise!"

"Lord, do not let us be melodramatic," retorted Don Camillo. "Why in the name of Heaven should it die? It's as pink and white as a rose!"

"Which means exactly nothing!" the Lord admonished him. "What if a tile should fall on its head, or it should suddenly have convulsions? It was your duty to baptize it."

Don Camillo raised protesting arms: "But, Lord, just think it over. If it were certain that the child would go to Hell we might stretch a point; but seeing that despite being the son of that nasty piece of work he might very easily manage to slip into Paradise, how can You ask me to risk anyone going there with such a name as Lenin? I'm thinking of the reputation of Paradise."

"The reputation of Paradise is My business," shouted the Lord angrily. "What matters to Me is that a man should be a decent fellow, and I care less than nothing whether his name be Lenin or Button. At the very most, you should have pointed out to those people that saddling children with fantastic names may involve them in annoyances when they grow up."

"Very well," replied Don Camillo. "I am always in the wrong. I must see what I can do about it."

Just at that moment someone came into the church. It was Peppone, alone, with the baby in his arms. He closed the church door and bolted it.

"I do not leave this church," he said, "until my son has been baptized with the name that I have chosen."

"Look at that," whispered Don Camillo, smiling as he turned towards the Lord. "Now do You see what these people are? One is filled with the holiest intentions and this is how they treat you."

"Put yourself in his place," replied the Lord. "One may not approve his attitude, but one can understand it."

Don Camillo shook his head.

"I have already said that I do not leave this place unless you baptize my son as I demand!" repeated Peppone. Whereupon, laying the bundle containing the baby upon a bench, he took off his coat, rolled up his sleeves and advanced threateningly.

"Lord," implored Don Camillo, "I ask You! If You think it just that one of Your priests should give way to the threats of a layman, then I must obey. But in that event, if to-morrow they should bring me a calf and compel me to baptize it You must not complain. You know very well how dangerous it is to create precedents."

"All right," replied the Lord, "but in this case you must try to make him understand. . . ."

"And if he hits me?"

"Then you must accept it. You must endure and suffer as I did."

Don Camillo turned to his visitor. "Very well, Peppone," he said. "The baby will leave the church baptized, but not by that accursed name."

"Don Camillo," stuttered Peppone, "don't forget that my stomach has never recovered from that bullet that I stopped in the mountains. If you hit low, I shall go for you with a bench."

"Don't worry, Peppone. I can deal with you entirely in the upper storeys," Don Camillo assured him, landing him a neat one above the ear.

They were both burly men with muscles of steel, and their blows fairly whistled through the air. After twenty minutes of silent and furious combat, Don Camillo distinctly heard a voice behind him. "Now, Don Camillo! The point of the jaw!" It came from the Lord above the altar.

Don Camillo struck hard, and Peppone crashed to the ground.

He remained where he lay for some ten minutes; then he sat up, got to his feet, rubbed his jaw, shook himself, put on his jacket and reknotted his red handkerchief. Then he picked up the baby. Fully vested, Don Camillo was waiting for him, steady as a rock, beside the font. Peppone approached him slowly.

"What am I to name him?" asked Don Camillo.

"Camillo Libero Antonio," muttered Peppone.

Don Camillo shook his head. "No; we will name him Libero Camillo Lenin," he said. "Yes, Lenin. When you have a Camillo around, such folk as he are quite helpless."

"Amen," muttered Peppone, gently prodding his jaw.

When all was done and Don Camillo passed before the altar the Lord smiled and remarked: "Don Camillo, I am bound to admit that in politics you are My master."

"And also in fisticuffs," replied Don Camillo, with perfect gravity, carelessly fingering a large lump on his forehead.

ON THE TRAIL

Don Camillo had let himself go a bit in the course of a little sermon with a local background, allowing himself some rather pointed allusions to *"certain people"*, and it was thus that on the following evening, when he seized the ropes of the church bells—the bell-ringer having been called away on some pretext—all hell broke out. Some damned soul had tied crackers to the clappers of the bells. No harm done, of course, but there was a shattering din of explosions, enough to give the ringer heart failure.

Don Camillo had not said a word. He had celebrated the evening service in perfect composure, before a crowded congregation from which not one was absent, with Peppone in the front row and every countenance a picture of fervour. It was enough to infuriate a saint, but Don Camillo was no novice in self-control, and his audience had gone home disappointed.

As soon as the big doors were closed Don Camillo snatched up an overcoat, and on his way out went to make a hasty genuflection before the altar.

"Don Camillo," said the Lord, "put it down."

"I don't understand," protested Don Camillo.

"Put it down!"

Don Camillo drew a heavy stick from beneath his coat and laid it in front of the altar.

"Not a pleasant sight, Don Camillo."

"But, Lord! It isn't even oak; it's only poplar, light and supple . . ." Don Camillo pleaded.

"Go to bed, Don Camillo, and forget about Peppone."

Don Camillo had raised his arms and had gone to bed with a temperature. And so when on the following evening Peppone's wife made her appearance at the presbytery he leaped to his feet as though a cracker had gone off under his chair.

"Don Camillo," began the woman, who was visibly greatly agitated.

But Don Camillo interrupted her. "Get out of my sight, sacrilegious creature!"

"Don Camillo, never mind about that foolishness. At Castellino there is that poor wretch who tried to do in Peppone! They have turned him out!"

Don Camillo lighted a cigar. "Well, what about it, comrade? I didn't make the amnesty. And in any case, why should you bother about it?"

The woman started to shout. "I'm bothering because they came to tell Peppone, and Peppone has gone rushing off to Castellino like a lunatic. And he has taken his tommy-gun with him!"

"I see; then you have got concealed arms, have you?"

"Don Camillo, never mind about politics! Can't you understand that Peppone is out to kill? Unless you help me my man is done for!"

Don Camillo laughed unpleasantly. "Which will teach him to tie crackers to the clappers of my bells. I shall be pleased to watch him die in gaol! You get out of my house!"

Ten minutes later, Don Camillo, with his skirts tucked up almost to his neck, was pedalling like a lunatic along the road to Castellino astride a racing bicycle belonging to the son of his sacristan.

There was a splendid moon, and when he was about four miles from Castellino, Don Camillo saw by its light a man sitting on the low parapet of the little bridge that spans the Fossone. He slowed down, since it is always best to be prudent when one travels at night, and halted some ten yards from the bridge, holding in his hand a small object that he happened to have discovered in his pocket.

"My son," he inquired, "have you seen a big man go by on a bicycle in the direction of Castellino?"

"No, Don Camillo," replied the other quietly.

Don Camillo drew nearer. "Have you already been to Castellino?" he asked.

"No. I thought it over. It wasn't worth while. Was it my fool of a wife who put you to this trouble?"

"Trouble? Nothing of the kind . . . a little constitutional!"

"Have you any idea what a priest looks like on a racing bicycle?" sniggered Peppone.

Don Camillo came and sat beside him on his wall. "My son, you must be prepared to see all kinds of things in this world."

64

Less than an hour later Don Camillo was back at the presbytery and went to make his report to the Lord.

"All went well according to Your instructions."

"Well done, Don Camillo, but would you mind telling me who it was that instructed you to take him by the feet and tumble him into the ditch?"

Don Camillo raised his arms. "To tell You the truth, I really can't remember exactly. As a matter of fact, he appeared to dislike the sight of a priest on a racing bicycle, so it seemed only kind to prevent him from seeing it any longer."

"I understand. Has he got back yet?"

"He'll be here soon. Seeing him fall into the ditch, it struck me that as he would be coming home in a rather damp condition he might find the bicycle in his way, so I thought it best to bring it along with me."

"Very kind of you, I'm sure, Don Camillo," said the Lord, with perfect gravity.

Peppone appeared just before dawn at the door of the presbytery. He was soaked to the skin, and Don Camillo asked if it was raining.

"Fog," replied Peppone, with chattering teeth. "May I have my bicycle?"

"Why, of course. There it is."

"Are you sure there wasn't a tommy-gun tied to it?"

Don Camillo raised his arms with a smile. "A tommy-gun? And what may that be?"

"I," said Peppone as he turned from the door, "have made one mistake in my life. I tied crackers to the clappers of your bells. It should have been half a ton of dynamite."

"Errare humanum est," remarked Don Camillo.

EVENING SCHOOL

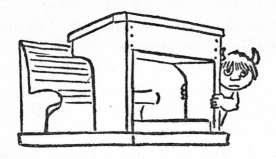

IN THE empty church, by the faint light of the two altar candles, Don Camillo was chatting with the Lord about the outcome of the local elections.

"I wouldn't presume to criticize Your actions," he wound up, "but I should never have allowed Peppone to become mayor with a council in which only two people really know how to read and write properly."

"Culture is entirely without importance, Don Camillo," replied the Lord with a smile. "What counts is ideas. Eloquent speeches get nowhere unless there are practical ideas at the back of them. Before judging, suppose we put them to the test."

"Fair enough," conceded Don Camillo. "I really said what I did because, in the event of the lawyer's Party coming out top, I had already been given assurances that the bell tower of the church would be repaired. In any case, should it fall down, the people will have compensation in watching the construction of a magnificent People's Palace with dancing, sale of alcoholic liquors, gambling and a theatre for variety entertainments."

"And a lock-up for such venomous reptiles as Don Camillo," added the Lord.

Don Camillo lowered his head. "Lord, You misjudge me," he said. "You know what a cigar means to me? Well, look: this is the only cigar I possess, and look what I am doing with it."

He pulled a cigar out of his pocket and crumbled it in his enormous hand.

"Well done," said the Lord. "Well done, Don Camillo. I accept your penance. Nevertheless, I should like to see you throw away the crumbs, because you would be quite capable of putting them in your pocket and smoking them later on in your pipe."

"But we are in church," protested Don Camillo.

"Never mind that, Don Camillo. Throw the tobacco into that corner."

Don Camillo obeyed while the Lord looked on with approval, and just then a knocking was heard at the little door of the sacristy and Peppone came in.

"Good evening, Mr. Mayor," said Don Camillo deferentially.

"Listen," said Peppone. "If a Christian is in doubt about something that he has done and comes to tell you about it, and if you found that he had made some mistakes, would you point them out to him, or would you simply leave him in ignorance?"

Don Camillo protested indignantly: "How can you dare to doubt the honesty of a priest? His primary duty is to point out clearly all the penitent's mistakes."

"Very well, then," exclaimed Peppone. "Are you quite ready to hear my confession?"

"I am ready."

Peppone pulled a large sheet of paper from his pocket and began to read: "Citizens, at the moment when we are hailing the victorious affirmation of our Party . . ."

Don Camillo interrupted him with a gesture and

went to kneel before the altar. "Lord," he murmured, "I am no longer responsible for my actions."

"But I am," said the Lord promptly. "Peppone has outwitted you, and you must play fair and do your duty."

"But, Lord," persisted Don Camillo, "You realize, don't You, that You are making me work on behalf of the Agit-Prop?"

"You are working on behalf of grammar, syntax and spelling, none of which is either diabolical or sectarian."

Don Camillo put on his spectacles, grasped a pencil and set to work on the tottering periods of the speech that Peppone was to make on the following day. Peppone read it through intently.

"Good," he approved. "There is only one thing that I do not understand. Where I had said: *'It is our intention to extend the schools and to rebuild the bridge over the Fossalto'*, you have substituted: *'It is our intention to extend the schools, repair the church tower and rebuild the bridge over the Fossalto.'* Why is that?"

"A mere matter of syntax," explained Don Camillo gravely.

"Blessed are those who have studied Latin and who are able to understand niceties of language," sighed Peppone. "And so," he added, "we are to lose even the hope that the tower may collapse on to your head!"

Don Camillo raised his arms. "We must all bow before the will of God!"

When he returned from accompanying Peppone to the door, Don Camillo came to say good night to the Lord.

"Well done, Don Camillo," said the Lord with a smile. "I was unjust to you, and I am sorry you destroyed your last cigar. It was a penance that you did not deserve. Nevertheless, we may as well be frank about it: Peppone was a skunk not to offer you even a cigar, after all the trouble you took!"

"Oh, all right," sighed Don Camillo, fishing a cigar from his pocket and preparing to crush it in his big hand.

"No, Don Camillo," smiled the Lord. "Go and smoke it in peace. You have earned it."

"But . . ."

"No, Don Camillo; you didn't steal it. Peppone had two cigars in his pocket. Peppone is a

Communist. He believes in sharing things. In skilfully relieving him of one cigar, you only took your fair share.''

"You always know best," exclaimed Don Camillo with deep respect.

OUT OF BOUNDS

ON CAMILLO was in the habit of going to measure the famous crack in the church tower, and every morning his inspection met with the same result: the crack had not increased in width, but neither had it diminished. Finally, he lost his temper, and one day he dispatched the sacristan to the headquarters of the commune.

"Go and tell the mayor to come at once and look at this damage. Explain that the matter is serious."

The sacristan went and returned.

"Peppone says that he will take your word for it that it is a serious matter. In any case, he also said that if you really want to show him the crack, you had better take the tower to him in his office. He will be available there until five o'clock."

Don Camillo did not bat an eyelid: all he said was: "If Peppone or any member of his gang has the courage to turn up at Mass to-morrow we shall see something sensational. But they know it, and not one of them will put in an appearance."

The next morning there was no sign of a Red in church, but five minutes before Mass was due to begin the sound of marching was heard upon the flags before the church door. In perfect formation all the Reds, not only those of the village but also those of neighbouring cells, every man jack of them, including the cobbler, Bilò, who had a wooden leg, and Roldo dei Prati, who was shivering with fever, came marching proudly towards the church, led by Peppone. With perfect composure they took their seats in church, sitting in a solid phalanx with faces as ferocious as the cruiser *Potemkin*.

When Don Camillo had finished his sermon, a very cultured exposition of the parable of the good Samaritan, he followed it by a brief exhortation to the faithful.

"As you all know, a most dangerous crack is threatening the security of the church tower. I therefore appeal to you, my dear brethren in the faith, to come to the assistance of the house of God. In using the term 'brethren in the faith' I am addressing those decent folk who come here with a desire to draw near to God, and not certain individuals who come only in order to parade their militarism. To such as these it can matter nothing should the tower fall to the ground.''

The Mass over, Don Camillo settled himself at a table near the presbytery door and the congregation filed past him, but not a soul left the place. One and all, having made the expected donation, remained on the little *piazzetta* in front of the church to watch developments. And last of all came Peppone, followed by his battalion in perfect formation. They drew up to a defiant halt before the table.

Peppone stepped forward proudly.

''From this tower, in the past, the bells have hailed the dawn of freedom, and from it, to-morrow, they shall welcome the glorious dawn of the proletarian revolution,'' said Peppone to Don Camillo as he laid on the table before him three large red handkerchiefs full of money.

Then he turned on his heel and marched away,

followed by his gang. And Roldo dei Prati was shaking with fever and could scarcely remain on his feet, but he held his head erect, and the crippled Bilò, as he passed Don Camillo, stamped his wooden leg defiantly in perfect step with his comrades.

When Don Camillo went to the Lord to show Him the basket containing the money and told Him that there was more than enough for the repair of the tower, the Lord smiled in astonishment.

"You were quite right, Don Camillo."

"Naturally," replied Don Camillo. "Because You understand humanity, but I know Italians."

Up to that moment Don Camillo had behaved well. But he made a mistake when he sent a message to Peppone to the effect that he had much admired the military smartness of his men, but that he advised him to give them more intensive drilling in right-about-turn and the double, of which they would have urgent need on the day of the proletarian revolution.

This was deplorable, and Peppone prepared to retaliate.

Don Camillo was an honest man, but in addition to an overwhelming passion for shooting he possessed a splendid double-barrelled gun and a good supply of cartridges. Moreover, Baron Stocco's private shoot lay only three miles from the village and constituted a permanent temptation, because not only game but even the neighbouring poultry had learned that they were in safety behind his fence of wire-netting and once within it could thumb their noses at anyone who wished to wring their necks.

It was therefore not at all astonishing that on a certain evening Don Camillo, his skirts bundled into an enormous pair of breeches and his face partly concealed beneath the brim of an ancient felt hat, should find himself actually on the business side of the Baron's fence. The flesh is weak, and the flesh of the sportsman particularly so.

Nothing to be surprised at, therefore, if Don Camillo fired a shot that brought down a hare almost under his nose. He thrust it into his game-bag and was beating a retreat when he suddenly found himself face to face with another invader. Ramming his hat down over his eyes, he butted the stranger in the stomach with the intention of knocking him out, since it was undesirable that the countryside should learn that their parish priest had been caught poaching.

Unfortunately, his adversary conceived the same idea at precisely the same moment and the two heads met with a crash so tremendous that both parties found themselves sitting on the ground seeing stars.

"A pate as hard as that can only belong to our beloved mayor," muttered Don Camillo as his vision began to clear.

"A pate as hard as that can only belong to our beloved parish priest," replied Peppone, scratching his head. For Peppone also was poaching on forbidden ground and also had a hare in his game-bag, and his eye gleamed as he surveyed Don Camillo.

"Never would I have believed," said Peppone, "that the very man who preaches respect for other people's property would be found breaking through the fences of a preserve in order to go poaching."

"Nor would I have believed that our chief citizen, our comrade mayor . . ."

"Citizen, yes, but also comrade," Peppone interrupted, "and therefore perverted by those diabolic theories that aim at the fair distribution of all property, and therefore acting more logically in accordance with his known views than the reverend Don Camillo, who, for his part . . ."

Someone was approaching them and had drawn so near that it was quite impossible to take to their heels without the risk of stopping a charge of shot, since on this occasion the intruder happened to be a gamekeeper.

"We've got to do something!" whispered Don Camillo. "Think of the scandal if we are recognized!"

"Personally, I don't care," replied Peppone, with composure. "I am always ready to answer for my actions."

The steps drew nearer, and Don Camillo melted against a large tree-trunk. Peppone made no attempt to move, and when the gamekeeper appeared with his gun over his arm Peppone greeted him:

"Good evening."

"What are you doing here?" inquired the gamekeeper.

"Looking for mushrooms."

"With a gun?"

"As good a means as another."

The means whereby a gamekeeper can be rendered relatively innocuous are also fairly simple. If one happens to be standing behind him it suffices to muffle his head unexpectedly in an overcoat and give him a good rap on the head. Advantage can then be taken of his moment of unconsciousness in order to reach the hedge and scramble over it. Once over, all is well.

Don Camillo and Peppone found themselves sitting behind a bush a good mile away from the Baron's estate.

"Don Camillo!" sighed Peppone. "We have committed a serious offence. We have raised our hands against one in authority! That is a felony."

Don Camillo, who had in point of fact been the one to raise them, broke out into a cold sweat.

"My conscience troubles me," pursued the tormentor. "I shall have no peace remembering so horrible a thing. How shall I dare present myself before a minister of God to ask forgiveness for such a misdeed? Accursed be the day when I lent an ear to the infamous lures of the Muscovite doctrine, forgetting the holy precepts of Christian charity!"

Don Camillo was so deeply humiliated that he wanted to cry. On the other hand, he also wanted desperately to land one good crack on the pate of his perverted adversary, and as Peppone was well aware of the fact, he left off.

"Accursed temptation!" he shouted suddenly, pulling the hare out of his bag and hurling it from him.

"Accursed indeed!" shouted Don Camillo, and, hauling out his own hare, he flung it far into the snow and walked away with bent head.

Peppone followed him as far as the cross-roads and then turned to the right. "By the way," he asked, pausing for a moment, "could you tell me of a reputable parish priest in this neighbourhood to whom I could go and confess this sin?"

Don Camillo clenched his fists and walked straight ahead.

When he had gathered sufficient courage to present himself before the Lord above the altar Don Camillo spread his arms wide.

"I didn't do it to save myself, Lord," he said. "I did it simply because, had it become known that I go poaching, the Church would have been the chief sufferer from the scandal."

But the Lord remained silent, and in such cases Don Camillo acquired a quartan ague and put himself on a diet of bread and water for days and days, until the Lord felt sorry for him and said: "Enough."

This time, the Lord said nothing until the bread-and-water diet had continued for seven days. Don Camillo had reached the stage where he could only remain standing by leaning against a wall, and his stomach was fairly bawling with hunger.

Then Peppone came to confession.

"I have sinned against the law and Christian charity," said Peppone.

"I know it," replied Don Camillo.

"Moreover, as soon as you were out of sight I went back and collected both the hares and I have roasted one and jugged the other."

"Just what I supposed you would do," murmured Don Camillo.

And when he passed the altar a little later the Lord smiled at him, not so much on account of his prolonged fast as in consideration of the fact that Don Camillo, when he had murmured, "Just what I supposed you would do," had felt no desire to hit Peppone but had experienced profound shame at the remembrance that on that same evening he himself had had a momentary temptation to do exactly the same thing.

"Poor Don Camillo!" whispered the Lord tenderly.

And Don Camillo spread out his arms as though he wished to say that he did his best and that if he sometimes made mistakes it was not deliberately.

"I know, I know, Don Camillo," replied the Lord. "And now get along and eat your hare—for Peppone has left it for you, nicely cooked, in the presbytery kitchen."

THE TREASURE

ONE DAY Smilzo made his appearance at the presbytery. He was a young ex-partisan who had been Peppone's orderly during the fighting in the mountains, and the latter had now taken him on as messenger to the commune. He was the bearer of a handsome letter printed in Gothic lettering on hand-made paper and with the Party heading.

"Your honour is invited to grace with his presence a ceremony of a social nature which will take place to-morrow at ten o'clock a.m. in Piazza della Libertà. The Secretary of the Section, Comrade Bottazzi, Mayor, Giuseppe."

Don Camillo looked severely at Smilzo. "Tell

Comrade Peppone Mayor Giuseppe that I have no wish to go and listen to the usual imbecilities against reaction and the capitalists. I already know them by heart."

"No," explained Smilzo. "This is no affair of political speeches. This is a question of patriotism and social activities. If you refuse it means that you know nothing of democracy."

Don Camillo nodded his head slowly. "If that is so," he said, "then I have nothing more to say."

"Very good. And the leader says you are to come in uniform and to bring all your paraphernalia."

"Paraphernalia?"

"Yes: the pail and the brush; there is something to be blessed."

Smilzo permitted himself to speak in such a manner to Don Camillo precisely because he was Smilzo—that is to say, the lean one, and so built that by virtue of his amazing swiftness of movement he had been able in the mountains to slip between bullet and bullet without coming to harm. By the time, therefore, that the heavy book flung at him by Don Camillo reached the spot where his head had been, Smilzo had already left the presbytery and was pedalling away for dear life.

Don Camillo got up, rescued the book and went to let off steam to the Lord at the altar.

"Lord," he said, "is it conceivable that I should be unable to find out what those people are planning to do to-morrow? I never knew anything so mysterious. What is the meaning of all these preparations? All those branches that they are sticking into the ground round the meadow between the pharmacy and the Baghettis' house? What kind of devilry can they be up to?"

"My son, if it were devilry, first of all they wouldn't be doing it in the open, and secondly they wouldn't be sending for you to bless it. Be patient until to-morrow."

That evening Don Camillo went to have a look round, but he saw nothing but branches and decorations surrounding the meadow and nobody appeared to know anything.

When he set out next morning, followed by two acolytes, his knees were trembling. He felt that something was not as it should be, that there was treachery in the air.

He returned an hour later, shattered and with a temperature.

"What has happened?" inquired the Lord from the altar.

"Enough to make one's hair stand on end," stammered Don Camillo. "A terrible thing. A band, Garibaldi's hymn, a speech from Peppone and the laying of the foundation stone of 'The People's Palace'! And I had to bless the stone while Peppone chuckled with joy. And the ruffian asked me to say a few words, and I had to make a suitable little address because, although it is a Party activity, the rascal dressed it up as a social undertaking."

Don Camillo paced to and fro in the empty church. Then he came to a standstill in front of the Lord. "A mere trifle," he exclaimed. "An assembly hall, reading-room, library, gymnasium, dispensary and theatre. A skyscraper of two floors with adjacent ground for sports and *bocce*. And the whole lot for the miserable sum of ten million lire."

"By no means dear, given the present prices," observed the Lord.

Don Camillo sank down upon a bench. "Lord,"

he sighed dolefully, "why have You done this to me?"

"Don Camillo, you are unreasonable."

"No: I am not unreasonable. For ten years I have been praying to You on my knees to find me a little money so that I could establish a library, an assembly hall for the young people, a playground for the children with a merry-go-round and swings and possibly a little swimming-pool like they have at Castellino. For ten years I have lowered myself making up to swine of bloated landowners when I should have liked to box their ears every time I saw them. I must have got up quite two hundred lotteries and knocked at quite two thousand doors, and I have nothing at all to show for it. Then along comes this excommunicate mountebank, and behold ten million lire drop into his pockets from heaven."

The Lord shook His head. "They didn't fall from heaven," He replied. "He found them underground. I had nothing to do with it, Don Camillo. It is entirely due to his own personal initiative."

Don Camillo spread out his arms. "Then it is simple enough, and the obvious deduction is that I am a poor fool."

Don Camillo went off to stamp up and down his study in the presbytery, roaring with fury. He must exclude the possibility that Peppone had got himself that ten million by holding people up on the roads or by robbing a bank. "That fellow in the days of the liberation, when he came down from the mountains and it seemed as if the proletarian revolution might break out at any moment, must have played upon the funk of those cowards of gentry and squeezed their money out of them."

Then he reflected that at that time there had been no gentry in the neighbourhood, but that, on the other hand, there had been a detachment of the British Army, which had arrived simultaneously with Peppone and his men. The British had taken possession of the gentry's houses, taking the place of the Germans, who, having spent some time in the countryside, had thoroughly cleared those houses of everything of any value. It was therefore out of the question that Peppone should have obtained his ten million by looting.

Possibly the money had come from Russia? He burst out laughing: was it likely that the Russians should give a thought to Peppone?

At last he returned to the church. "Lord," he

begged from the foot of the altar, "won't You tell me where Peppone found the money?"

"Don Camillo," replied the Lord with a smile, "do you take Me for a private detective? Why ask God to tell you the truth when you have only to seek it within yourself? Look for it, Don Camillo, and meanwhile, in order to distract your mind, why not make a trip to the town?"

On the following evening, having returned from his excursion to the town, Don Camillo presented himself before the Lord in a condition of extreme agitation.

"What has upset you, Don Camillo?"

"Something quite crazy," explained Don Camillo breathlessly. "I have met a dead man! Face to face in the street!"

"Don Camillo, calm yourself and reflect: usually the dead whom one meets face to face in the street are alive."

"This one cannot be!" shouted Don Camillo. "This one is dead as mutton, and I know it because I myself carried him to the cemetery."

"If that is the case," replied the Lord, "then I have nothing more to say. You must have seen a ghost."

Don Camillo shrugged his shoulders. "Of course not! Ghosts have no existence except in the foolish pates of hysterical women!"

"And therefore?"

"Well . . ." muttered Don Camillo.

Don Camillo collected his thoughts. The deceased had been a thin young man, not a native of the village, who had come down from the mountains with Peppone and his men. He had been wounded in the head and was in a bad state, and they had fixed him up in the former German headquarters, which had become the headquarters of the British Command. Peppone had established his own office in the room next to that of the invalid. Don Camillo remembered it all clearly: the villa was surrounded by sentries three deep and not a fly could leave it unperceived, because the British were still fighting nearby and were particularly careful of their own skins.

All this had happened one morning, and on the same evening the young man had died. Peppone had sent for Don Camillo towards midnight, but by the time he had got there the young man had been already in his coffin. The British didn't want the body in the house, and so, at about noon, the coffin, covered with the Italian flag, was carried out of the villa by Peppone and his most trusted men. A detachment of British soldiers had kindly volunteered to supply military honours.

Don Camillo recalled that the ceremony had been moving: all the village had walked behind the coffin, which had been placed on a gun-carriage. He himself had made the address before the body was lowered into the grave, and people had actually wept. Peppone, in the front row, had sobbed.

"When I put my mind to it, I certainly know how to express myself!" said Don Camillo to himself complacently, recalling the episode. Then he returned to his original train of thought. "And in spite of all that, I am prepared to take my oath that the young man whom I met to-day in the town was the same as the one I followed to the grave." He sighed. "Such is life!"

The following day Don Camillo sought out Peppone at his workshop, where he found him lying on his back underneath a car.

"Good morning, Comrade Mayor. I have come to tell you that for the past two days I have been thinking over your description of your People's Palace!"

"And what do you think of it?" jeered Peppone.

"Magnificent! It has made me decide to start work on that scheme of a little place with a bathing-pool, garden, sports-ground, theatre, etcetera, which, as you know, I have had in mind for twenty years past. I shall be laying the foundation stone next Sunday. It would give me great pleasure if you, as mayor, would attend the ceremony."

"Willingly: courtesy for courtesy."

"In the meanwhile, you might try to cut down the plans for your own place a bit. It looks like being too big for my personal taste."

Peppone stared at him in amazement. "Don Camillo, are you demented?"

"No more than I was when I conducted a funeral and made a patriotic address over a coffin that can't have been securely closed, because only yesterday I met the corpse walking about the town."

Peppone ground his teeth. "What are you trying to insinuate?"

"Nothing: only that that coffin to which the British presented arms was full of what you found in the cellars of the Villa Dotti, where the German

Command had hidden it. And that the dead man was alive and concealed in the attic."

"A-a-h!" howled Peppone. "The same old story! An attempt to malign the partisan movement!"

"Leave the partisans out of it. I take no interest in them!"

And he walked away while Peppone stood muttering vague threats.

That same evening, Don Camillo was awaiting him at the presbytery when he arrived accompanied by Brusco and two other prominent supporters—the same men who had acted as coffinbearers.

"You," said Peppone, "can drop your insinuations. It was all of it stuff looted by the Germans—silver, cameras, instruments, gold, etcetera. If we hadn't taken it, the British would have had it. Ours was the only possible means of getting it out of the place. I have here witnesses and receipts: nobody has touched so much as a lira. Ten million was taken and ten million will be spent for the people."

Brusco, who was hot-tempered, began to shout that it was God's truth and that he, if necessary, knew well enough how to deal with certain people.

"So do I," Don Camillo replied calmly. He dropped the newspaper which he had been holding extended in front of himself and thus allowed it to be seen that under his right arm-pit he held the famous tommy-gun that had once belonged to Peppone.

Brusco turned pale and retreated hastily, but Peppone extended his arms. "Don Camillo, it doesn't seem to me that there is any need to quarrel."

"I agree," replied Don Camillo. "The more easily as I am entirely of your opinion. Ten million was acquired and ten million should be spent on the people. Seven on your People's Palace and three on my recreation centre for the people's children. 'Suffer the little children to come unto Me.' I ask only what is my due."

The four consulted together for a moment in undertones. Then Peppone spoke: "If you hadn't got that damnable thing in your hands, I should tell you that your suggestion is the filthiest blackmail in the universe."

On the following Sunday, Peppone, together

with all the village council, assisted at the laying of the foundation stone of Don Camillo's recreation centre. He also made a short speech. However, he found a means of whispering in Don Camillo's ear: "It might be better to tie this stone round your neck and throw you into the Po."

That evening Don Camillo went to make his report to the Lord above the altar.

"Well, what do You think about it?" he said in conclusion.

"Exactly what Peppone said to you. That if you hadn't got that damnable thing in your hands I should say that it was the filthiest blackmail in the universe."

"But I have nothing at all in my hands except the cheque that Peppone has just given me."

"Precisely," whispered the Lord. "And with that three million you are going to do so many beautiful things, Don Camillo, that I haven't the heart to scold you."

Don Camillo genuflected and went off to bed to dream of a garden full of children—a garden with a merry-go-round and a swing, and seated on the swing Peppone's youngest son chirping joyfully like a fledgling.

RIVALRY

A BIG noise from the town was expected on a visit, and people were coming from all the surrounding cells. Therefore Peppone decreed that the ceremony should be held in the big square, and he not only had a large platform, decorated with red, set up, but he got hold of one of those trucks with four great loudspeakers and all the electric mechanism inside them for amplifying the voice. And so, on the afternoon of that Sunday, the big square was crammed to overflowing with people, and so also was the church square, which happened to be adjacent.

Don Camillo had shut all the doors and with-drawn into the sacristy, so as to avoid seeing or hearing anything which would work him up into a temper. He was actually dozing when a voice like the wrath of God roused him with a jerk as it bellowed: *"Comrades! . . ."*

It was as though the walls had melted away.

Don Camillo went to work off his indignation at the high altar. "They must have aimed one of their accursed loudspeakers directly at the church," he exclaimed. "This is nothing short of violation of domicile."

"What can you do about it, Don Camillo? It is progress," replied the Lord.

After a preface of generalizations, the voice had got down to business and, since the speaker was an extremist, he made no bones about it.

"We must remain within the law, and we shall do so! Even at the cost of taking up our weapons and of using the firing-squad for all the enemies of the people! . . ."

Don Camillo was pawing the ground like a restive horse. "Lord, only listen to him!"

"I hear him, Don Camillo. I hear him only too well."

"Lord, why don't You drop a thunderbolt among all that rabble?"

"Don Camillo, let us remain within the law. If,

in order to drive the truth into the head of one who is in error, your remedy is to shoot him down, where was the use of My allowing Myself to be crucified?"

Don Camillo threw up his hands. "You are right, of course. We can do nothing but wait for them to crucify us also."

The Lord smiled. "If, instead of speaking first and then thinking over what you have said, you thought first and did the speaking afterwards, you might avoid having to regret the foolish things you have said."

Don Camillo bowed his head.

"... *as for those who, hiding in the shadow of the Crucifix, attempt with the poison of their ambiguous words to spread dissension among the masses of the workers* ..." The voice of the loudspeaker, borne on the wind, filled the church and shook the blue, red and yellow glass in the gothic windows. Don Camillo grasped a heavy bronze candlestick and, brandishing it like a club, strode with clenched teeth in the direction of the church door.

"Don Camillo, stop!" cried the Lord. "You will not leave the church until everyone has gone away."

"Oh, very well," replied Don Camillo, putting

back the candlestick in its place. "I obey." He strode up and down the church and finally halted in front of the Lord. "But in here I can do as I please?"

"Naturally, Don Camillo; here you are in your own house and free to do exactly as you wish. Short of climbing up to a window and firing at the people below."

Three minutes later, Don Camillo, leaping and bounding cheerfully in the bell-chamber of the church tower, was performing the most infernal carillon that had ever been heard in the village.

The orator was compelled to interrupt his speech and turned to the local authorities who were standing with him on the platform. "He must be stopped!" he cried indignantly.

Peppone agreed gravely, nodding his head. "He must indeed," he replied, "and there are just two ways of stopping him. One is to explode a mine under the church tower, and the other is to bombard it with heavy artillery."

The orator ordered him to stop talking nonsense. Surely it was easy enough to break in the door of the tower and climb the stairs.

"Well," said Peppone calmly, "one goes up by

ladders from landing to landing. Look, comrade, do you see those projections just by the big window of the belfry? They are the steps that the bell-ringer has removed as he went up. By closing the trap-door of the top landing, he is cut off from the world."

"We might try firing at the windows of the tower," suggested Smilzo.

"Certainly," agreed Peppone; "but we should have to be certain of knocking him out with the first shot, otherwise he also would begin firing, and then there might be trouble."

The bells ceased ringing and the orator resumed his speech, and all went well only so long as he was careful to say nothing of which Don Camillo disapproved. If he did so, Don Camillo immediately began the counter-argument with his bells, leaving off only to resume as soon as the orator left the straight and narrow path again. And so on until the peroration was merely pathetic and patriotic and was therefore respected by the admonitory bells.

That evening Peppone met Don Camillo. "Take care, Don Camillo, that this baiting does not bring you to a bad end."

"There is no baiting involved," replied Don

Camillo calmly. "You blow your trumpets and we ring our bells. That, comrade, is democracy. If, on the other hand, only one person is allowed to perform, that is a dictatorship."

Peppone held his peace, but one morning Don Camillo got up to find a merry-go-round, a swing, three shooting-galleries, an electric track, the "wall of death" and an indefinite number of other booths established within exactly half a yard of the line that divided the church square from the public square.

The owners of the "amusement park" showed him their permits, duly signed by the mayor, and Don Camillo retired without comment to his presbytery. That evening pandemonium broke out: barrel organs, loudspeakers, gunfire, shouting and singing, bells, whistling, roaring, braying and bellowing.

Don Camillo went to protest before the Lord. "This is a lack of respect towards the house of God."

"Is there anything about it that is immoral or scandalous?" asked the Lord.

"No—merry-go-rounds, swings, little motor cars, chiefly children's amusements."

"Well, then, it is simply democracy."

"But this infernal din?" protested Don Camillo.

"The din also is democracy, provided it remains within the law. Outside church territory, the mayor is in command, my son."

The presbytery stood some thirty yards further forward than the church, having one of its sides adjoining the square, and exactly underneath one of its windows a strange apparatus had been erected that immediately aroused Don Camillo's curiosity. It was a kind of small column about three feet high, topped by a sort of stuffed mushroom covered with leather. Behind it was another column, taller and more slender, upon which was a large dial bearing figures from 1 to 1000. It was an instrument for the trial of strength: a blow was struck at the mushroom and the dial recorded its force. Don Camillo, squinting through the cracks of the shutters, began to enjoy himself. By eleven o'clock in the evening the highest number recorded was 750, and that stood to the credit of Badile, the Grettis' cowman, who had fists like sacks of potatoes. Then quite suddenly Comrade Peppone made his appearance, surrounded by his satellites.

All the people came running to see, crying, "Go on, Peppone. Go to it!" And Peppone removed his jacket, rolled up his sleeves and took his stand opposite the machine, measuring the distance with his clenched fist. There was total silence, and even Don Camillo felt his heart hammering.

Peppone's fist cleft the air and struck the mushroom.

"Nine hundred and fifty," yelled the owner of the machine. "Only once before have I seen any man get that score, and he was a longshoreman in Genoa." The crowd howled with enthusiasm.

Peppone put on his coat again, raised his head and looked at the window behind which Don Camillo was concealed. "To anyone whom it may concern," he remarked loudly, "I might say that a blow that registers nine hundred and fifty is no joke!"

Everyone looked up at Don Camillo's window and sniggered.

Don Camillo went to bed with his legs shaking under him. On the next evening he was there again, watching from behind his window and waiting feverishly for the clock to strike eleven. Once again Peppone arrived with his staff, took off his coat, rolled up his sleeve and aimed a mighty blow at the mushroom.

"Nine hundred and fifty-one!" howled the crowd. And once again they looked up at Don Camillo's window and sniggered. Peppone also looked up.

"To anyone whom it may concern," he remarked loudly, "I might say that a blow that registers nine hundred and fifty-one is no joke!"

Don Camillo went to bed that night with a temperature.

Next day he went and knelt before the Lord. "Lord," he sighed, "I am being dragged over the precipice!"

"Be strong and resist, Don Camillo!"

That evening Don Camillo went to his peep-hole in the window as though he were on his way to the scaffold. Rumour had spread like wildfire and the whole countryside had come to see the performance. When Peppone appeared there was an audible whisper of "Here he is!" Peppone looked up, jeering, took off his coat, raised his fist and there was silence.

"Nine hundred and fifty-two!"

Don Camillo saw a million eyes fixed upon his

window, lost the light of reason and hurled himself out of the room.

"To anyone whom . . ." Peppone did not have time to finish his remarks about a blow that registered nine hundred and fifty-two: Don Camillo already stood before him. The crowd bellowed, and then was suddenly silent.

Don Camillo threw out his chest, took a firm stance, threw away his hat and crossed himself. Then he raised his formidable fist and struck hard.

"One thousand!" yelled the crowd.

"To anyone whom it may concern, I might say that a blow that registers one thousand is no joke," remarked Don Camillo.

Peppone had grown rather pale, and his satellites were glancing at him doubtfully, hesitating between resentment and disappointment. Other bystanders were chuckling delightedly. Peppone looked Don Camillo straight in the eyes and took off his coat again. He stepped in front and raised his fist.

"Lord!" whispered Don Camillo hastily.

Peppone's fist cleft the air.

"A thousand," bawled the crowd, and Peppone's bodyguard rejoiced.

"At one thousand all blows are formidable,"

observed Smilzo. "I think we will leave it at that."

Peppone moved off triumphantly in one direction while Don Camillo moved off triumphantly in the other.

"Lord," said Don Camillo when he knelt before the crucifix. "I thank You. I was scared to death."

"That you wouldn't make a thousand?"

"No; that that pig-headed fool wouldn't make it too. I should have had it on my conscience."

"I knew it; and it was lucky that I came to your help," replied the Lord, smiling. "Moreover, Peppone also, as soon as he saw you, nearly died of fear lest you shouldn't succeed in reaching nine hundred and fifty-two."

"Possibly!" muttered Don Camillo, who now and then liked to appear sceptical.

CRIME AND PUNISHMENT

ON Easter morning, Don Camillo, leaving his home at an early hour, was confronted at the door of the presbytery by a colossal chocolate egg tied up with a handsome riband of red silk. Or, rather, by a formidable egg that resembled a chocolate one, but was merely a two-hundred-pound bomb shorn of its fins and painted a rich brown.

The war had not omitted to pass over Don Camillo's parish, and planes had visited it on more than one occasion, dropping bombs. A number of these had remained unexploded, half buried in the ground or actually lying on the surface, since the planes had flown low. When all was over, a couple of engineers had arrived from somewhere or other, exploded the bombs lying far from any building and dismantled those too close to occupied places. These they had collected to be disposed of later. One bomb had fallen upon the old mill, destroying the roof and remaining wedged between a wall and a main beam, and it had been left there because the house was derelict. It was this bomb that had been transformed into an Easter egg by unknown hands.

"Unknown," let us say, as a figure of speech, since there was the inscription: "Happy Eester" (with two e's), and there was also the red riband. The business had been carefully organized, because when Don Camillo turned his eyes away from the strange egg he found the church square thronged with people. These scoundrels had all conspired to be present in order to enjoy Don Camillo's discomfiture.

Don Camillo felt annoyed and allowed himself to kick the object, which, naturally, remained immovable.

"It's pretty heavy!" someone shouted.

"Needs the bomb-removal squad!" suggested another voice.

There was a sound of sniggering.

"Try blessing it and see if it doesn't walk off of its own accord!" cried a third voice.

Don Camillo went pale and his knees began to tremble. Slowly he bent down and with his immense hands grasped the bomb at its two extremities. There was a deathly silence. The crowd gazed at Don Camillo, holding their breaths, their eyes staring in something akin to fear.

"Lord!" whispered Don Camillo desperately.

"Heave ho, Don Camillo!" replied a quiet voice that came from the high altar.

The bones of that great frame literally cracked. Slowly and implacably Don Camillo straightened his back with the enormous mass of iron welded to his hands. He stood for a moment contemplating the crowd and then he set out. Every step fell like a ton weight. He left the church square and step by step, slow and inexorable as Fate, Don Camillo crossed the big square. The crowd followed in silence, amazed. On reaching the far end of the square, opposite the Party headquarters, he stopped. And the crowd also stopped.

"Lord," whispered Don Camillo desperately.

"Heave ho, Don Camillo!" came a rather

anxious voice from the now-distant high altar of the church.

Don Camillo collected himself, then in one sudden movement he brought the great weight up to the level of his chest. Another effort and the bomb began slowly to rise higher, watched by the now-frightened crowd.

Now Don Camillo's arms were fully extended and the bomb poised above his head. For one moment he held it there, then he hurled it from him and it landed on the ground exactly in front of the door of the Party headquarters.

Don Camillo looked at the crowd. "Returned to sender," he observed in a ringing voice. "Easter is spelt with an A. Correct and re-deliver."

The crowd made way for him, and Don Camillo returned triumphantly to the presbytery.

Peppone did not re-deliver the bomb. With two helpers he loaded it on to a cart and it was removed and thrown down a disused quarry at a distance from the village. The bomb rolled down a slope but did not reach the bottom, because it was arrested by a tree-stump and remained wedged in an upright position.

Three days later it happened that a goat

approached the quarry and discovered an alluring patch of fresh grass at the roots of the tree-stump. In cropping the grass, it pushed the bomb, which resumed its descent and, having travelled some two yards, struck a stone and exploded with terrific violence. In the village, at a considerable distance, the windows of thirty houses were shattered.

Peppone arrived at the presbytery a few moments later, gasping, and found Don Camillo going up-stairs.

"And to think," groaned Peppone, "that I spent an entire evening hammering at those fins!"

"And to think that I . . ." moaned Don Camillo, and could get no further, because he was visualizing the scene in the square.

"I'm going to bed . . ." gasped Peppone.

"I was on my way there . . ." gasped Don Camillo.

He had the crucifix from the high altar brought to him in his bedroom.

"Forgive me if I put You to this inconvenience," murmured Don Camillo, whose temperature was raging, "but I had to thank You on behalf of the whole village."

"No need of that, Don Camillo," replied the Lord with a smile. "No need of that."

One morning shortly after this, on leaving the house, Don Camillo discovered that during the night someone had defaced the white wall of the presbytery by writing upon it in red letters two feet high the words: *Don Camàlo*, which means stevedore, and undoubtedly referred to his recent feat of strength.

With a bucket of whitewash and a large brush Don Camillo set to work to efface the inscription, but in view of the fact that it was written in aniline red, the application of whitewash was completely useless and the letters only glared more balefully through any number of coats. Don Camillo had to resort to scraping, and the job took him quite half the day.

He made his appearance before the Lord above the altar as white as a miller all over but in a distinctly black frame of mind. "If I can only find out who did it," he said, "I shall thrash him until my stick is worn away."

"Don't be melodramatic, Don Camillo," the Lord advised him. "This is some urchin's doing. After all, no one has really insulted you."

"Do You think it seemly to call a priest a stevedore?" protested Don Camillo. "And then, it's the kind of nickname that, if people get hold of it, may stick to me all my life."

"You've got broad shoulders, Don Camillo," the Lord consoled him, with a smile. "I never had shoulders like yours and yet I bore the Cross without beating anybody."

Don Camillo agreed that the Lord was in the right. But he was not satisfied, and that evening, instead of going to his bed, he took up his station in a strategic position and waited patiently. Towards two o'clock in the morning an individual made his appearance in the church square and, having placed a small pail on the ground beside him, set to work carefully upon the wall of the presbytery. But without giving him time even to complete the letter D, Don Camillo overturned the pail on his head and sent him flying with a terrific kick in the pants.

Aniline dye is an accursed thing, and Gigotto (one of Peppone's most valued henchmen), on receiving the baptism of red paint, remained for three days concealed in his house scrubbing his face with every conceivable concoction, after which he was compelled to go out and work. The facts had already become generally known, and he found himself greeted with the nickname of "Redskin".

Don Camillo fanned the flames until a day came when, returning from a visit to the doctor, he discovered too late that the handle of his front door had received a coating of red. Without uttering so much as one word, Don Camillo went and sought out Gigotto at the tavern and with a blow that was enough to blind an elephant liberally daubed his face with the paint collected from the door-handle. Naturally, the occurrence immediately took on a political aspect and, in view of the fact that Gigotto was supported by half a dozen of his own party, Don Camillo was compelled to use a bench in self-defence.

The six routed by the bench were seething with fury. The tavern was in an uproar, and the same evening some unknown person serenaded Don Camillo by throwing a firework in front of the presbytery door.

People were getting anxious and it needed but a

spark to set fire to the tinder. And so, one fine morning, Don Camillo received an urgent summons to the town because the bishop wished to speak to him.

The bishop was old and bent, and in order to look Don Camillo in the face he had to raise his head considerably. "Don Camillo," said the bishop, "you are not well. You need to spend a few months in a beautiful mountain village. Yes, yes; the parish priest at Puntarossa has died recently, and so we shall kill two birds with one stone: you will be able to reorganize the parish for me and at the same time you will re-establish your health. Then you will come back as fresh as a rose. You will be supplied by Don Pietro, a young man who will make no trouble for you. Are you pleased, Don Camillo?"

"No, Monsignore; but I shall leave as soon as Monsignore wishes."

"Good," replied the bishop. "Your discipline is the more meritorious inasmuch as you accept without discussion my instructions to do something that is against your personal inclinations."

"Monsignore, you will not be displeased if the

people of my parish say that I have run away because I was afraid?"

"No," replied the old man, smiling. "Nobody on this earth could ever think that Don Camillo was afraid. Go with God, Don Camillo, and leave benches alone; they can never constitute a Christian argument."

The news spread quickly in the village. Peppone had announced it in person at a special meeting. "Don Camillo is going," he proclaimed. "Transferred to some God-forsaken mountain village. He is leaving to-morrow afternoon at three o'clock."

"Hurrah!" shouted the entire meeting. "And may he croak when he gets there. . . ."

"All things considered, it's the best way out," said Peppone. "He was beginning to think he was the King and the Pope rolled into one, and if he had stayed here we should have had to give him a super dressing-down. This saves us the trouble."

"And he should be left to slink away like a whipped cur," howled Brusco. "Make the village understand that there will be trouble for anyone who is seen about the church square from three to half-past."

The hour struck and Don Camillo went to say good-bye to the Lord above the altar. "I wish I could have taken You with me," sighed Don Camillo.

"I shall go with you just the same," replied the Lord. "Don't you worry."

"Have I really done anything bad enough to deserve being sent away?" asked Don Camillo.

"Yes."

"Then they really are all against me," sighed Don Camillo.

"All of them," replied the Lord. "Even Don Camillo himself disapproves of what you have done."

"That is true enough," Don Camillo acknowledged. "I could hit myself."

"Keep your hands quiet, Don Camillo, and a pleasant journey to you."

In a town fear can affect 50 per cent of the people, but in a village the percentage is doubled. The roads were deserted. Don Camillo climbed into the train, and when he watched his church tower disappear behind a clump of trees he felt very bitter indeed. "Not even a dog has remembered me," he sighed. "It is obvious that I have failed in my duties and it is also obvious that I am a bad lot."

The train was a slow one that stopped at every station, and it therefore stopped at Boschetto, a mere cluster of four houses three or four miles from Don Camillo's own village. And so, quite suddenly, Don Camillo found his compartment invaded; he was hustled to the window and found himself face to face with a sea of people who were clapping their hands and throwing flowers.

"Peppone's men had said that if anyone in the village showed up at your departure it meant a hiding," the steward from Stradalunga was explaining, "and so, in order to avoid trouble, we all came on here to say good-bye to you."

Don Camillo was completely dazed and felt a humming in his ears and when the train moved off the entire compartment was filled with flowers, bottles, bundles and parcels of all sizes, while poultry with their legs tied together clucked and protested from the baggage-nets overhead.

But there was still a thorn in his heart. "And

those others? They must really hate me to have done such a thing! It wasn't even enough for them to get me sent away!"

A quarter of an hour later the train stopped at Boscoplanche, the last station of the commune. There Don Camillo heard himself called by name, and going to the window beheld Mayor Peppone and his entire *giunta*. Mayor Peppone made the following speech:

"Before you leave the territory of the commune, it seems to us proper to bring you the greetings of the population and good wishes for a rapid recovery, the which will enable a speedy return to your spiritual mission."

Then, as the train began to move, Peppone took off his hat with a sweeping gesture and Don Camillo also removed his hat and remained standing at the window with it posed in the air like a statue of the Risorgimento.

The church at Puntarossa sat on the top of the mountain and looked like a picture postcard. When Don Camillo reached it he inhaled the pine-scented air deeply and exclaimed with satisfaction:

"A bit of rest up here will certainly do me good,

the which will enable a speedy return to my spiritual mission."

And he said it quite gravely, because to him that "the which" was of more value than the sum of all Cicero's orations.

RETURN TO THE FOLD

THE PRIEST who had been sent to supply the parish during Don Camillo's political convalescence was young and delicate. He knew his business and he spoke courteously, using lovely, polished phrases that appeared to be newly minted. Naturally, even though he knew that he was only in temporary occupation, this young priest established some small changes in the church such as any man feels to be necessary if he is to be tolerably at his ease in strange surroundings.

We are not making actual comparisons, but it is much the same when a traveller goes to an hotel. Even if he is aware that he will remain there only for one night he will be inclined to move a table from left to right and a chair from right to left, because each one of us has a strictly personal concept of æsthetic balance and colour and experiences discomfort on every occasion when, being at liberty to do so, he does not exert himself to create such harmony as he desires.

It therefore happened that on the first Sunday following the new priest's arrival the congregation noticed two important innovations: the great candlestick that supported the big paschal candle with its floral decorations and which had always stood on the second step at the Gospel side of the altar had been shifted to the Epistle side and placed in front of a small picture representing a saint—a picture which had previously not been there.

Out of curiosity, together with respect to the new parish priest, the entire village was present, with Peppone and his henchmen in the foremost ranks.

"Have you noticed," muttered Brusco to Peppone with a stifled snigger, pointing out the candlestick, "changes?"

"M-m-m," mumbled Peppone irritably. And he remained irritable until the priest came down to the altar rails to make the customary address.

Then Peppone could bear no more, and just as the priest was about to begin he detached himself from his companions, marched steadily towards the candlestick, grasped it firmly, carried it past the altar and placed it in its old position upon the second step to the left. Then he returned to his seat in the front row and with knees wide apart and arms folded stared arrogantly straight into the eyes of the young priest.

"Well done!" murmured the entire congregation, not excepting Peppone's political opponents.

The young priest, who had stood open-mouthed watching Peppone's behaviour, changed colour, stammered somehow through his brief address and returned to the altar to complete his Mass.

When he left the church he found Peppone waiting for him with his entire staff. The church square was crowded with silent and surly people.

"Listen here, Don—Don whatever you call yourself," said Peppone in an aggressive voice. "Who is this new person whose picture you have hung on the pillar to the right of the altar?"

"Santa Rita da Cascia," stammered the little priest.

"Then let me tell you that this village has no use

for Santa Rita da Cascia or anything of the kind. Here everything is better left as it was before."

The young priest spread out his arms. "I think I am entitled . . ." he began, but Peppone cut him short.

"Ah, so that's how you take it? Well, then let us speak clearly: this village has no use for a priest such as you."

The young priest gasped. "I cannot see that I have done anything . . ."

"Then I'll tell you what you have done. You have committed an illegal action. You have attempted to change an order that the permanent priest of the parish had established in accordance with the will of the people."

"Hurrah!" shouted the crowd, including the reactionaries.

The little priest attempted a smile. "If that is all the trouble, everything shall be put back exactly as it was before. Isn't that the solution?"

"No," thundered Peppone, flinging his hat behind him and placing his enormous fists on his hips.

"And may I be allowed to ask why?"

Peppone had reached the end of his supplies of diplomacy. "Well," he said, "if you really want to know, it is not a solution because if I give you one on the jaw I shall send you flying at least fifteen yards, while if it were the regular incumbent he wouldn't move so much as an inch!''

Peppone stopped short of explaining that in the event of his hitting Don Camillo once, the latter would have hit him half a dozen times in return. He left it at that, but his meaning was clear to all his hearers with the exception of the little priest, who stared at him in amazement.

"But, excuse me," he murmured. "Why should you have any wish to hit me?"

Peppone lost patience. "Who in the world wants to hit you? There you are again, running down the left-wing parties! I used a figure of speech merely in order to explain our views. Is it likely that I should waste my time hitting a scrap of a priest like you?"

On hearing himself termed a "scrap of a priest", the young man drew himself up to his full five feet four inches and his face grew purple till the very veins in his neck swelled.

" 'Scrap of a priest' you may call me," he cried in a shrill voice, "but I was sent here by ecclesiastical authority and here I shall remain until ecclesiastical authority sees fit to remove me. In this church you have no authority at all! Santa Rita will stay where she is and, as for the candlestick, watch what I am going to do!"

He went into the church, grasped the candlestick firmly and after a considerable struggle succeeded in removing it again to the Epistle side of the altar in front of the new picture.

"There!" he said triumphantly.

"Very well!" replied Peppone, who had observed his actions from the threshold of the church door. Then he turned to the crowd which stood in serried ranks in the church square, silent and surly, and shouted: "The people will have something to say to this! To the town hall, all of you, and we will make a demonstration of protest."

"Hurrah!" howled the crowd.

Peppone elbowed his way through them so that he could lead them, and they formed up behind him yelling and brandishing sticks. When they reached the town hall the yells increased in volume, and Peppone yelled also, raising his fist and shaking it at the balcony of the council chamber.

"Peppone," shouted Brusco in his ear, "are you

crazy? Stop yelling! Have you forgotten that you yourself are the mayor?"

"Hell! . . ." exclaimed Peppone. "When these accursed swine make me lose my head I remember nothing!" He ran upstairs and out on to the balcony, where he was cheered by the crowd, including the reactionaries.

"Comrades, citizens," shouted Peppone. "We will not suffer this oppression that offends against our dignity as free men! We shall remain within the bounds of the law so long as may be possible, but we are going to get justice even if we must resort to gunfire! In the meantime I propose that a committee of my selection shall accompany me to the ecclesiastical authorities and impose in a democratic manner the desires of the people!"

"Hurrah!" yelled the crowd, completely indifferent to logic or syntax. "Long live our Mayor Peppone!"

When Peppone and his committee stood before the bishop he had some difficulty in finding his voice, but at last he got going.

"Excellence," he said, "that priest that you have sent us is not worthy of the traditions of the leading parish of the district."

The bishop raised his head in order to see the top of Peppone. "Tell me now: what has he been doing?"

Peppone waved his arms. "For the love of God! Doing? He hasn't done anything serious. . . . In fact, he hasn't done anything at all. . . . The trouble is that . . . Oh, well, Eminence, he's only a half-man . . . you know what I mean, a priestling; when the fellow is all dressed up—your Eminence must excuse me, but he looks like a coat-hanger loaded with three overcoats and a cloak!"

The old bishop nodded his head gravely. "But do you," he inquired very graciously, "establish the merits of priests with a tape measure and a weighing machine?"

"No, Excellence," replied Peppone. "We aren't savages! But all the same, how shall I put it—even the eye needs some satisfaction, and in matters of religion it's the same as with a doctor, there's a lot to be said for personal sympathies and moral impressions!"

The old bishop sighed. "Yes, yes. I understand perfectly. But all the same, my dear children, you had a parish priest who looked like a tower and you yourselves came and asked me to remove him!"

Peppone wrinkled his forehead. "Monsignore," he explained solemnly, "it was a question of a *casus belli*, an affair *sui generis*, as they say. Because that man was a multiple offence in the way he exasperated us by his provocative and dictatorial poses."

"I know, I know," said the bishop. "You told me all about it when you were here before, my son, and, as you see, I removed him. And that was precisely because I fully understood that I had to deal with an unworthy man. . . ."

"One moment, if you will excuse me," Brusco interrupted. "We never said that he was an unworthy man! . . ."

"Well, well; if not 'an unworthy man'," continued the bishop, "at any rate an unworthy priest, inasmuch as . . ."

"I beg your pardon," said Peppone, interrupting him. "We never suggested that as a priest he had failed in his duty. We only spoke of his serious defects, of his very serious misdeeds as a man."

"Exactly," agreed the old bishop. "And as, unfortunately, the man and the priest are inseparable, and a man such as Don Camillo represents a danger to his neighbours, we are at this very moment considering the question of making his present appointment a permanent one. We will leave him where he is, among the goats at Puntarossa. Yes, we will leave him there, since it has not yet been decided whether he is to be allowed to continue in his functions or whether we shall suspend him *a divinis*. We will wait and see."

Peppone turned to his committee and there was a moment's consultation, then he turned again to the bishop.

"Monsignore," he said in a low voice, and he was sweating and had gone pale, as though he found difficulty in speaking audibly, "if the ecclesiastical authority has its own reasons for doing such a thing, of course that is its own affair. Nevertheless, it is my duty to warn your Excellency that until our regular parish priest returns to us, not a soul will enter the church."

The bishop raised his arms. "But, my sons," he exclaimed, "do you realize the gravity of what you are saying? This is coercion!"

"No, Monsignore," Peppone explained, "we are coercing nobody, because we shall all remain quietly at home, and no law compels us to go to

church. Our decision is simply a question of avail-
ing ourselves of democratic liberty. Because we
are the only persons qualified to judge whether a
priest suits us or not, since we have had to bear
with him for nearly twenty years."

"*Vox populi vox Dei*," sighed the old bishop.
"God's will be done. You can have your reprobate back if you want him. But don't come whin-
ing to me later on about his arrogance."

Peppone laughed. "Eminence! The rodomon-
tades of a type such as Don Camillo don't really
break any bones. We came here before merely as a
matter of simple political and social precaution, so
as to make sure that Redskin here didn't lose his
head and throw a bomb at him."

"Redskin yourself!" retorted the indignant
Gigotto, whose face Don Camillo had dyed with
aniline red and whose head had come in contact with
Don Camillo's bench. "I never meant to throw any
bombs. I simply threw a firework in front of his
house to make him realize that I wasn't standing for
being knocked on the head even by the reverend
parish priest in person."

"Ah! Then it was you, my son, who threw the
firework?" inquired the old bishop indifferently.

"Well, Excellence," mumbled Gigotto, "you know how it is. When one has been hit on the head with a bench one may easily go a bit too far in retaliation."

"I understand perfectly," replied the bishop, who was old and knew how to take people in the right way.

Don Camillo returned ten days later.

"How are you?" inquired Peppone, meeting him just as he was leaving the station. "Did you have a pleasant holiday?"

"Well, it was a bit dreary up there. Luckily, I took my pack of cards with me and worked off my restlessness playing patience," replied Don Camillo. He pulled a pack of cards from his pocket. "Look," he said. "But now I shan't need them any more." And delicately, with a smile, he tore the pack in two as though it were a slice of bread.

"We are getting old, Mr. Mayor," sighed Don Camillo.

"To hell with you and with those who sent you back here!" muttered Peppone, turning away, the picture of gloom.

Don Camillo had a lot to tell the Lord above the altar. Then at the end of their gossip he inquired, with an assumption of indifference:

"What kind of a fellow was my supply?"

"A nice lad, cultured and with a nice nature. When anyone did him a good turn, he didn't bait them by tearing up a pack of cards under their noses."

"Lord!" exclaimed Don Camillo, raising his arms. "I don't suppose anyone here ever did him a good turn, anyway. And then there are people who have to be thanked like that. I'll bet You that now Peppone is saying to his gang: 'And he tore the whole pack across, zip, the misbegotten son of an ape!' And he is thoroughly enjoying saying it! Shall we have a wager?"

"No," replied the Lord with a sigh; "because that is exactly what Peppone is saying at this moment."

THE DEFEAT

THE WAR to the knife that had now been in process for nearly a year was won by Don Camillo, who managed to complete his recreation centre while Peppone's People's Palace still lacked all its locks.

The recreation centre proved to be a very up-to-date affair: a hall for social gatherings, dramatic performances, lectures and such-like activities, a library with a reading- and writing-room and a covered area for physical training and winter games. There was in addition a magnificent fenced sports-ground with a gymnasium, running-track, bathing-pool and a children's playground with giant-stride, swings, etcetera. Most of the paraphernalia was as yet in an embryonic stage, but the important thing was to have made a start.

For the inauguration ceremony Don Camillo had prepared a most lively programme: choral singing, athletic competitions and a game of football. For the latter Don Camillo had succeeded in mustering a really formidable team, a task to which he had brought so impassioned an enthusiasm that in the course of the team's eight months of training the kicks administered by him alone to the eleven players were far more numerous than those that all those players put together had succeeded in giving to the ball.

Peppone knew all this and was deeply embittered. He could not endure the thought that the Party that genuinely represented the people must play second fiddle in the celebration organized by Don Camillo on the people's behalf. And when Don Camillo sent to inform him that in order to demonstrate his "sympathetic understanding of the more ignorant social strata of the village" he was willing to allow a match between their Dynamos football team and his own Galliards, Peppone turned pale, summoned the eleven lads of the local sports squadron and made them stand to attention against the wall while he made them the following address: "You are to play against the priest's team. You have got to win or I shall smash in every one of your faces. The Party orders it for the honour of a downtrodden people!"

"We shall win!" replied the eleven, sweating with terror.

As soon as this scene was reported to him Don Camillo mustered the Galliards and addressed them as follows.

"We are not here among uncouth savages such as your opponents," he said, smiling pleasantly. "We are capable of reasoning like sensible and educated gentlemen. With the help of God, we shall beat them six goals to none. I make no threats; I merely remind you that the honour of the parish is in your hands. Also in your feet.

"Therefore let each of you do his duty as a good citizen. Should there be some Barabbas among you who is not ready to give his all even to the last drop of his blood, I shall not indulge in Peppone's histrionics with regard to the smashing of faces. I shall merely kick his backside to a jelly!"

The entire countryside attended the inauguration, led by Peppone and his satellites with blazing red handkerchiefs round their necks. In his capacity as *mayor*, he expressed his satisfaction at the event, and as *personal representative of the people* he emphasized his confident belief that the occasion they were celebrating would not be made to serve "unworthy ends of political propaganda such as were already being whispered of by ill-intentioned persons".

During the performance of the choral singers, Peppone was able to point out to Brusco that, as a matter of fact, singing was also a sport, inasmuch as it developed the expansion of the lungs, and Brusco, with seeming amiability, replied that in his opinion the exercise would prove even more efficacious as a means of physical development for Catholic youth if they were taught to accompany it with gestures adapted to the improvement not only of their lung power, but also of the muscles of their arms.

During the game of basket-ball Peppone expressed a sincere conviction that the game of ping-pong also not only had an undeniable athletic value, but was so graceful that he was astonished not to find it included in the programme.

In view of the fact that these comments were made in voices that were easily audible half a mile away, the veins of Don Camillo's neck were very soon swollen to the size of cables. He therefore awaited with indescribable impatience the hour of the football match, which would be that of his reply.

At last it was time for the match. White jerseys with a large "G" on the breast for the eleven Galliards. Red jerseys bearing the hammer, sickle and star combined with an elegant "D" adorned the eleven Dynamos.

The crowd cared less than nothing for symbols, anyway, and hailed the teams after their own fashion: "Hurrah for Peppone!" or "Hurrah for Don Camillo!" Peppone and Don Camillo looked at one another and exchanged slight and dignified bows.

The referee was a neutral: the clockmaker Binella, a man without political opinions. After ten minutes' play the sergeant of carabinieri, pale to the gills, approached Peppone, followed by his two equally pallid subordinates.

"Mr. Mayor," he stammered, "don't you think it would be wise for me to telephone to the town for reinforcements?"

"You can telephone for a division for all I care, but

if those butchers don't let up, nobody will be able to avoid there being a heap of corpses as high as the first-floor windows! Not His Majesty the King himself could do a thing about it, do you understand?" howled Peppone, forgetting the very existence of the republic in his blind fury.

The sergeant turned to Don Camillo, who was standing a few feet away. "Don't you think . . .?" he stuttered, but Don Camillo cut him short.

"I," he shouted, "simply think that nothing short of the personal intervention of the United States of America will prevent us all from swimming in blood if those accursed bolsheviks don't stop disabling my men by kicking them in the shins!"

"I see," said the sergeant, and went off to barricade himself into his quarters, although perfectly aware that the common sequel of such behaviour is a general attempt to close the festivities by setting fire to the barracks of the carabinieri.

The first goal was scored by the Galliards and raised a howl that shook the church tower. Peppone, his face distorted with rage, turned on Don Camillo with clenched fists as though about to attack him. Don Camillo's fists were already in position. The two of them were within a hair's-breadth of conflict, but Don Camillo observed out of the tail of his eye that all other eyes present were fixed upon them.

"If we begin fighting there'll be a free-for-all," he muttered through clenched teeth to Peppone.

"All right, for the sake of the people."

"For the sake of the faith," said Don Camillo.

Nothing happened. Nevertheless, Peppone, when the first half ended a few moments later, mustered the Dynamos. "Fascists!" he said to them in a voice thick with contempt. Then, seizing hold of Smilzo, the centre-forward: "As for you, you dirty traitor, suppose you remember that when we were in the mountains I saved your worthless skin no less than three times. If in the next five minutes you haven't scored a goal, I'll attend to that same skin of yours!"

Smilzo, when play was resumed, got the ball and set to work. And work he did, with his head, with his legs and with his knees. He even bit the ball, he spat his lungs out and split his spleen, but at the fourth minute he sent the ball between the posts.

Then he flung himself on to the ground and lay motionless. Don Camillo moved over to the other side of the ground lest his self-control should fail him. The Galliards' goalkeeper was in a high fever from sheer funk.

The Dynamos closed up into a defensive phalanx that seemed impregnable. Thirty seconds before the end the referee whistled and a penalty was given against the Galliards. The ball flew into the air. A child of six could not have muffed it at such an angle. Goal!

The match was now over. The only task remaining for Peppone's men was that of picking up their injured players and carrying them back to their pavilion. The referee had no political views and left them to it.

Don Camillo was bewildered. He ran off to the church and knelt in front of the altar. "Lord," he said, "why did You fail to help me? I have lost the match."

"And why should I have helped you rather than the others? Your men had twenty-two legs and so had they, Don Camillo, and all legs are equal. Moreover, they are not My business. I am interested in souls. *Da mihi animam, caetera tolle.* I leave the bodies on earth. Don Camillo, where are your brains?"

"I can find them with an effort," said Don Camillo. "I was not suggesting that You should have taken charge of my men's legs, which in any case were the best of the lot. But I do say that You did not prevent the dishonesty of one man from giving a foul unjustly against my team."

"The priest can make a mistake in saying Mass, Don Camillo. Why must you deny that others may be mistaken while being in good faith?"

"One can admit of errors in most circumstances, but not when it is a matter of arbitration in sport! When the ball is actually there . . . Binella is a scoundrel . . ." He was unable to continue because at that moment the sound of an imploring voice became progressively audible and a man came running into the church, exhausted and gasping, his face convulsed with terror.

"They want to kill me," he sobbed. "Save me!"

The crowd had reached the church door and was about to irrupt into the church itself. Don Camillo seized a candlestick weighing half a quintal and brandished it menacingly.

"Back, in God's name, or I strike!" he shouted. "Remember that anyone who enters here is sacred and immune!"

The crowd hesitated.

"Shame on you, you pack of wolves! Get back to your lairs and pray God to forgive you your savagery."

The crowd stood in silence, heads were bowed, and there was a general movement of retreat.

"Make the sign of the Cross," Don Camillo ordered them severely, and as he stood there brandishing the candlestick in his huge hand he seemed a very Samson.

Everyone made the sign of the Cross.

"Between you and the object of your brutality is now that sign of the Cross that each one of you has traced with his own hand. Anybody who dares to violate that sacred barrier is a blasphemer. *Vade retro!*" He himself stood back and closed the church door, drawing the bolt, but there was no need.

The fugitive had sunk on to a bench and was still panting. "Thank you, Don Camillo," he murmured.

Don Camillo made no immediate reply. He paced to and fro for a few moments and then pulled up opposite the man. "Binella!" said Don Camillo in accents of fury. "Binella, here in my presence and that of God you dare not lie! There was no foul! How much did that reprobate Peppone give you to make you call a foul in a drawn game?"

"Two thousand five hundred lire."

"M-m-m-m!" roared Don Camillo, thrusting his fist under his victim's nose.

"But then . . ." moaned Binella.

"Get out," bawled Don Camillo, pointing to the door.

Once more alone, Don Camillo turned towards the Lord. "Didn't I tell You that the swine had sold himself? Haven't I a right to be enraged?"

"None at all, Don Camillo," replied the Lord. "You started it when you offered Binella two thousand lire to do the same thing. When Peppone bid five hundred lire more, Binella accepted the higher bribe."

Don Camillo spread out his arms. "Lord," he said, "but if we are to look at it that way, then I emerge as the guilty man!"

"Exactly, Don Camillo. When you, a priest, were the first to make the suggestion, he assumed that there was no harm in the matter, and then, quite naturally, he took the more profitable bid."

Don Camillo bowed his head. "And do You

mean to tell me that if that unhappy wretch should get beaten up by my men it would be my doing?"

"In a certain sense, yes, because you were the first to lead him into temptation. Nevertheless, your sin would have been greater if Binella, accepting your offer, had agreed to cheat on behalf of your team. Because then the Dynamos would have done the beating up and you would have been powerless to stop them."

Don Camillo reflected awhile. "In fact," he said, "it was better that the others should win."

"Exactly, Don Camillo."

"Then, Lord," said Don Camillo, "I thank You for having allowed me to lose. And if I tell You that I accept the defeat as a punishment for my dishonesty You must believe that I am really penitent. Because, to see a team such as mine who might very well—and I am not bragging—play in Division B, a team that, believe me or not, could swallow up and digest a couple of thousand Dynamos in their stride, to see them beaten . . . is enough to break one's heart and cries for vengeance to God!"

"Don Camillo!" the Lord admonished him, smiling.

"You can't possibly understand me," sighed Don Camillo. "Sport is a thing apart. Either one cares or one doesn't. Do I make myself clear?"

"Only too clear, my poor Don Camillo. I understand you so well that . . . Come now, when are you going to have your revenge?"

Don Camillo leaped to his feet, his heart swelling with delight. "Six to nothing!" he shouted. "Six to nought that they never even see the ball! Do You see that confessional?"

He flung his hat into the air, caught it with a neat kick as it came down and drove it like a thunderbolt into the little window of the confessional.

"Goal!" said the Lord, smiling.

THE AVENGER

SMILZO RODE up on his racing bicycle and braked it in the American manner, which consists of letting the backside slip off the seat backwards and sit astride the wheel.

Don Camillo was reading the newspaper, seated upon the bench in front of the presbytery. He raised his head. "Does Stalin hand you down his trousers?" he inquired placidly.

Smilzo handed him a letter, touched his cap with a forefinger, leaped on to his bicycle and was just about to disappear round the corner of the presbytery when he slowed down for an instant. "No, the Pope does that," he bawled, then stood on his pedals and was gone in a flash.

Don Camillo had been expecting the letter. It contained an invitation to the inauguration ceremony of the People's Palace with a programme of the festivities enclosed. Speeches, reports, a band and refreshments. Then, in the afternoon: *"Great Boxing Match between the Heavyweight Champion of the Local Section, Comrade Bagotti Mirco, and the Heavyweight Champion of the Provincial Federation, Comrade Gorlini Anteo."*

Don Camillo went off to discuss the event with the Lord above the altar. "Lord!" he exclaimed when he had read the programme aloud. "If this isn't vile! If Peppone hadn't been an utter boor he would have staged the return match between the Galliards and the Dynamos instead of this pummelling bout! And so I shall . . ."

"And so you will not even dream of going to tell him one word of what you would like to say; and in any case you're entirely wrong," the Lord interrupted him. "It was perfectly logical of Peppone to try to do something different. Secondly, it was also logical that Peppone should not expose himself to inaugurating his venture with a defeat. Even if we suppose that his champion may lose, he would be none the worse: one comrade fights another; it all remains in the family. But a defeat of his team by yours would be detrimental to the prestige of his Party. Don Camillo, you must admit that Peppone couldn't possibly have staged a return match against your team."

"And yet," exclaimed Don Camillo, "I did stage a match against his team, and what's more, I lost it!"

"But, Don Camillo," put in the Lord gently, "you don't represent a party. Your lads were not defending the colours of the Church. They were merely defending the prestige of a sporting team, of a pleasant combination that had been organized under the patronage of the parish church. Or do you perhaps think that that Sunday afternoon defeat was a defeat for the Catholic faith?"

Don Camillo began laughing. "Lord," he protested, " You wrong me if You accuse me of any such idea. I was only saying, as a sportsman, that Peppone is a boor. And so You will forgive me if I can't help laughing when his famous champion gets such a drubbing that by the third round he won't know his own name."

"Yes, I shall forgive you, Don Camillo. But I shall find it less easy to forgive your taking pleasure in the spectacle of two men belabouring each other with their fists."

Don Camillo raised his arms. "I have never done anything of the kind and would never lend my presence to countenance such manifestations of brutality as serve only to foster that cult of violence which is already too deeply rooted in the minds of the masses. I am in full agreement with You in condemning any sport in which skill is subordinated to brute force."

"Bravo, Don Camillo," said the Lord. "If a man feels the need to limber his muscles it is not necessary to fight with his neighbour. It suffices if, having put on a pair of well-padded gloves, he takes it out on a sack of sawdust or a ball suspended somewhere."

"Exactly," agreed Don Camillo, crossing himself hastily and hurrying away.

"Will you satisfy my curiosity, Don Camillo?" exclaimed the Lord. "What is the name of that leather ball which you have had fixed with elastic to the ceiling and the floor of your attic?"

"I believe it is called a 'punching ball'," muttered Don Camillo, halting for a moment.

"And what does that mean?"

"I don't know any English," replied Don Camillo, making good his escape.

Don Camillo attended the inaugural ceremony of the People's Palace and Peppone accompanied him personally upon a tour of the entire concern: it was all obviously thoroughly up-to-date.

"What do you think of it?" asked Peppone, who was burbling with joy.

"Charming!" replied Don Camillo, smiling cordially. "To tell you the truth, I should never have thought that it could possibly have been designed by a simple builder such as Brusco."

"True enough!" muttered Peppone, who had spent God only knew how much in order to have his project realized by the best architect in the town.

"Quite a good idea to make the windows horizontal instead of perpendicular," observed Don Camillo. "The rooms can be less lofty without its being too obvious. Excellent. And this I suppose is the warehouse."

"It is the assembly room," Peppone explained.

"Ah! And have you put the armoury and the cells for dangerous adversaries in the basement?"

"No," replied Peppone. "We haven't any dangerous adversaries; they are all harmless little folk that can remain in circulation. As for an armoury, we thought that in case of need we could make use of yours."

"An admirable idea," agreed Don Camillo politely. "You have been able to see for yourself how well I look after the tommy-gun which you entrusted to my care, Mr. Mayor."

They had pulled up in front of a huge picture representing a man with a heavy walrus moustache, small eyes and a pipe.

"Is that one of your dead leaders?" inquired Don Camillo respectfully.

"That is someone who is among the living and who when he comes will drive you to sit on the lightning conductor of your own church," explained Peppone, who had reached the end of his tether.

"Too high a position for a humble parish priest. The highest position in a small community always pertains to the mayor, and from now onwards I put it at your complete disposal."

"Are we to have the honour of your presence among us at the boxing match to-day, reverend sir?" asked Peppone, thinking it best to change the subject.

"Thank you, but you had better give my seat to

someone who is better qualified than I am to appreciate the innate beauty and deeply educational significance of the performance. But I shall at any rate be available at the presbytery in the event of your champion requiring the Holy Oils. You have only to send Smilzo, and I can be with you within a couple of minutes."

During the afternoon Don Camillo chatted for an hour with the Lord and then asked to be excused: "I am sleepy and I shall take a nap. And I thank You for making it rain cats and dogs. The crops needed it."

"And, moreover, according to your hopes, it will prevent many people coming from any distance to see Peppone's celebrations," added the Lord. "Am I right?"

Don Camillo shook his head.

The rain, heavy though it was, had done no harm at all to Peppone's festivities: people had flocked from every section of the countryside and from all the nearer communes, and the gymnasium of the People's Palace was as full as an egg. "Champion of the Federation" was a fine title, and Bagotti was undeniably popular in the region. And then it was also in some sense a match between town and country, and that aroused interest.

Peppone, in the front row close under the ring, surveyed the crowd triumphantly. Moreover, he was convinced that, at the worst, Bagotti could only lose on points, which, in such circumstances, would be almost as good as a victory.

On the stroke of four o'clock, after an outburst of applause and yelling sufficient to bring down the roof, the gong was sounded and the audience began to get restless and excitable.

It became immediately apparent that the provincial champion surpassed Bagotti in style, but on the other hand Bagotti was quicker, and the first round left the audience breathless. Peppone was pouring with sweat and appeared to have swallowed dynamite.

The second round began well for Bagotti, who took the offensive, but quite suddenly he went down in a heap and the referee began the count.

"No," bawled Peppone, leaping to his feet. "It was below the belt!"

The federal champion smiled sarcastically at Peppone. He shook his head and touched his chin with his glove.

"No!" bellowed Peppone in exasperation, drowning the uproar of the audience. "You all saw it! First he hit him low and when the pain made him double up he gave him the left on the jaw! It was a foul!"

The federal champion shrugged his shoulders and sniggered, and meanwhile the referee, having counted up to ten, was raising the victor's hand to show that he had won when the tragedy occurred.

Peppone flung away his hat and in one bound was in the ring and advancing with clenched fists upon the federal champion. "I'll show you," he howled.

"Give it to him, Peppone!" yelled the infuriated audience.

The boxer put up his fists and Peppone fell upon him like a Panzer and struck hard. But Peppone was too furious to retain his judgment, and his adversary dodged him easily and landed him one directly on the point of the jaw. Nor did he hesitate to put all his weight into it, as Peppone stood there motionless and completely uncovered: it was like hitting a sack of sawdust.

Peppone slumped to the ground and a wave of dismay struck the audience and smote them to a frozen silence. But just as the champion was smiling compassionately at the giant lying prone on the mat, there was a terrific yell from the crowd as a man entered the ring. Without even troubling to remove a drenched waterproof or his cap, he seized a pair of gloves lying on a stool in the corner, pulled them on without bothering to secure them and, standing on guard squarely before the champion, aimed a terrific blow at him. The champion dodged it, naturally, but failed to get in a return, as his opponent was ready for him. The champion danced round the man, who did no more than revolve slowly, and at a given moment the champion launched a formidable blow. The other seemed barely to move, but with his left he parried while his right shot forward like a thunderbolt. The champion was already unconscious as he fell, and lay as if asleep in the middle of the ring.

The audience went crazy.

It was the bell-ringer who brought the news to the presbytery, and Don Camillo had to leave his bed in order to open the door because the sacristan appeared to be insane and, had he not been allowed to pour out the whole story from A to Z, there seemed every reason for fearing that he might blow up. Don Camillo went downstairs to report to the Lord.

"Well?" the Lord inquired. "And how did it go off?"

"A very disgraceful brawl; such a spectacle of disorder and immorality as can hardly be imagined!"

"Anything like that business when they wanted to lynch your referee?" asked the Lord indifferently.

Don Camillo laughed. "Referee, my foot! At the second round Peppone's champion slumped like a sack of potatoes. Then Peppone himself jumped into the ring and went for the victor. Naturally, since, although he is strong as an ox, he is such a dunderhead that he pitches in without judgment, like a Zulu or a Russian, the champion gave him one on the jaw that laid him out like a ninepin."

"And so this is the second defeat his section has suffered."

"Two for the section and one for the federation," chuckled Don Camillo. "Because that was not the end! No sooner had Peppone gone down than another man jumped into the ring and fell upon the victor. Must have been somebody from one of the neighbouring communes, I imagine, a fellow with a beard and a moustache who put up his fists and struck out at the federal champion."

"And I suppose the champion dodged and struck back and the bearded man went down also and added his quotum to the brutal exhibition," the Lord remarked.

"No! The man was as impregnable as an iron safe. So the champion began dodging round trying to catch him off-guard, and finally, zac! he puts in a straight one with his right. Then I feinted with the left and caught him square with the right and left the ring!"

"And what have you to do with it?"

"I don't understand."

"You said: 'I feinted with the left and caught him square with the right'."

"I can't imagine how I came to say such a thing."

The Lord shook His head. "Could it possibly be because you yourself were the man who struck down the champion?"

"It would not seem so," said Don Camillo gravely. "I have neither beard nor moustache."

"But those, of course, could be assumed so that

the crowd should not suspect that the parish priest is interested in the spectacle of two men fighting in public with their fists?"

Don Camillo shrugged. "All things are possible, Lord, and we must also bear in mind that even parish priests are made of flesh and blood."

The Lord sighed. "We are not forgetting it, but we should also remember that if parish priests are made of flesh and blood they themselves should never forget that they are also made of brains. Because if the flesh-and-blood parish priest wishes to disguise himself in order to attend a boxing match, the priest that is made of brains prevents him from giving an exhibition of violence."

Don Camillo shook his head. "Very true. But You should also bear in mind that parish priests, in addition to flesh and blood and brains, are also made of yet another thing. And so, when that other thing sees a mayor sent flat on the mat before all his own people by a swine from the town who has won by striking below the belt (which is a sin that cries to heaven for vengeance), that other thing takes the priest of flesh and blood and the priest of brains by the throat and sends the lot of them into the ring."

The Lord nodded. "You mean to say that I should bear in mind that parish priests are also made of heart?"

"For the love of heaven," exclaimed Don Camillo. "I should never presume to advise You. But I would venture to point out that none of those present is aware of the identity of the man with the beard."

"Nor am I aware of it," replied the Lord with a sigh; "but I should like to know whether you have any idea of the meaning of those words 'punching ball'?"

"My knowledge of the English language has not improved, Lord," replied Don Camillo.

"Well, then we must be content without knowing even that," said the Lord, smiling. "After all, culture in the long run often seems to do more harm than good. Sleep well, federal champion."

NOCTURNE WITH BELLS

F<small>OR SOME</small> time Don Camillo had felt that he was being watched. On turning round suddenly when he was walking along the street or in the fields he saw no one, but felt convinced that if he had looked behind a hedge or among the bushes he would have found a pair of eyes and all that goes with them.

When leaving the presbytery on a couple of evenings he had not only heard a sound from behind the door, but he caught a glimpse of a shadow.

"Let it be," the Lord had replied from above the altar when Don Camillo had asked Him for advice. "Eyes never did anyone any harm."

"But it would be useful to know whether those

two eyes are going about alone or accompanied by a third, for instance one of 9-calibre," sighed Don Camillo. "That is a detail not without its own importance."

"Nothing can defeat a good conscience, Don Camillo."

"I know, Lord," sighed Don Camillo once more, "but the trouble is that people don't usually fire at a conscience, but between the shoulders."

However, Don Camillo did nothing about the matter and a little time elapsed, and then late one evening, when he was sitting alone in the presbytery reading, he unexpectedly "felt" the eyes upon him.

There were three of them, and raising his head slowly he saw first of all the black eye of a revolver and then those of Biondo.

"Do I lift my hands?" inquired Don Camillo quietly.

"I don't want to do you any harm," replied Biondo, thrusting the revolver into his jacket pocket. "I was afraid you might be scared when I appeared unexpectedly and might start shouting."

"I understand," replied Don Camillo. "And did it never strike you that by simply knocking at the door you could have avoided all this trouble?"

Biondo made no reply; he went and leaned over the window-sill. Then he turned round suddenly and sat down beside Don Camillo's little table. His hair was ruffled, his eyes deeply circled and his forehead was damp with sweat.

"Don Camillo," he muttered from behind clenched teeth, "that fellow at the house near the dyke; it was I that did him in."

Don Camillo lighted a cigar. "The house near the dyke?" he said quietly. "Well, that's an old story; it was a political affair and came within the terms of amnesty. What are you worrying about? You're all right under the law."

Biondo shrugged his shoulders. "To hell with the amnesty," he said furiously. "Every night when I put my light out I can feel him near my bed, and I can't understand what it means."

Don Camillo puffed a cloud of blue smoke into the air. "Nothing at all, Biondo," he replied, with a smile. "Listen to me: go to sleep with the light on."

Biondo sprang to his feet. "You can go and jeer at that fool Peppone," he shouted, "but you can't do it to me!"

Don Camillo shook his head. "Firstly, Peppone

is not a fool; and secondly, where you are concerned, there is nothing that I can do for you."

"If I must buy candles or make an offering to the church, I'll pay," shouted Biondo, "but you've got to absolve me. And in any case I'm all right legally!"

"I agree, my son," said Don Camillo mildly. "But the trouble is that no one has ever yet made an amnesty for consciences. Therefore, so far as we are concerned, we muddle along in the same old way, and in order to obtain absolution it is necessary to be penitent and then to act in a manner that is deserving of forgiveness. It's a lengthy affair."

Biondo sniggered. "Penitent? Penitent of having done in that fellow? I'm only sorry I didn't bag the lot!"

"That is a province in which I am completely incompetent. On the other hand, if your conscience tells you that you acted rightly, then you should be content," said Don Camillo, opening a book and laying it in front of Biondo. "Look, we have very clear rules that do not exclude the political field. Fifth: thou shalt not kill. Seventh: thou shalt not steal."

"What has that got to do with it?" inquired Biondo in a mystified voice.

"Nothing," Don Camillo reassured him, " but I had an idea that you told me that you had killed him, under the cloak of politics, in order to steal his money."

"I never said so!" shouted Biondo, pulling out his revolver and thrusting it into Don Camillo's face. "I never said so, but it's true! And if you dare to tell a living soul I shall blow you to pieces!"

"We don't tell such things even to the Eternal Father," Don Camillo reassured him; "and in any case He knows them better than we do."

Biondo appeared to quiet down. He opened his hand and looked at his weapon. "Now look at that!" he exclaimed, laughing. "I hadn't even noticed that the safety-catch was down."

He raised the catch with a careful finger.

"Don Camillo," said Biondo in a strange voice, "I am sick of seeing that fellow standing near my bed. There are only two ways for it: either you absolve me or I shoot you." The revolver shook slightly in his hand and Don Camillo turned rather pale and looked him straight in the eyes.

"Lord," said Don Camillo mentally, "this is a

mad dog and he will fire. An absolution given in such conditions is valueless. What do I do?"

"If you are afraid, give him absolution," replied the voice of the Lord.

Don Camillo folded his arms on his breast.

"No, Biondo," said Don Camillo.

Biondo set his teeth. "Don Camillo, give me absolution or I fire."

"No."

Biondo pulled the trigger and the trigger yielded, but there was no explosion.

And then Don Camillo struck, and his blow did not miss the mark, because Don Camillo's punches never misfired.

Then he flung himself up the steps of the tower and rang the bells furiously for twenty minutes. And all the countryside declared that Don Camillo had gone mad, with the exception of the Lord above the altar, who shook His head, smiling, and Biondo, who, tearing across the fields like a lunatic, had reached the bank of the river and was about to throw himself into its dark waters. Then he heard the bells.

So Biondo turned back because he had heard a

Voice that he had never known. And that was the real miracle, because a revolver that misfires is a material event, but a priest who begins to ring joy-bells at eleven o'clock at night is quite another matter.

MEN AND BEASTS

LA GRANDE was an enormous farm with a hundred cows, steam dairy, orchards and all the rest of it. And everything belonged to old Pasotti, who lived alone at the Badia with an army of retainers. One day these retainers set up an agitation and, led by Peppone, went *en masse* to the Badia and were interviewed by old Pasotti from a window.

"May God smite you," he shouted, thrusting out his head. "Can't a decent man have peace in this filthy country?"

"A decent man, yes," replied Peppone, "but not profiteers who deny their workmen what is their just due."

"I only admit of dues as fixed by the law," retorted Pasotti, "and I am perfectly within the law."

Then Peppone told him that so long as he refused to grant the concessions demanded, the workers of La Grande would do no work of any kind or description. "So you can feed your hundred cows yourself!" Peppone concluded.

"Very well," replied Pasotti. He closed the window and resumed his interrupted slumbers.

This was the beginning of the strike at La Grande, and it was a strike organized by Peppone in person, with a squad of overseers, regular watches, pickets and barricades. The doors and windows of the cowsheds were nailed up and seals placed upon them.

On the first day the cows lowed because they had not been milked. On the second day they lowed because they had not been milked and because they were hungry, and on the third day thirst was added to all the rest and the lowing could be heard for miles around. Then Pasotti's old servant came out by the back door of the Badia and explained to the men on picket duty that she was going in to the village to the pharmacy to buy disinfectants. "I have told the master that he can't possibly want to get cholera from the stench when all the cows have died of starvation."

This remark caused quite a lot of head-shaking among the older labourers, who had been working for more than fifty years for Pasotti and who knew that he was incredibly pig-headed. And then Peppone himself stepped in to say, with the support of his staff, that if anyone dared to go near the cowshed he would be treated as a traitor to his country.

Towards the evening of the fourth day, Giacomo, the old cowman from La Grande, made his appearance at the presbytery.

"There is a cow due to calve and she is crying out fit to break your heart, and she will certainly die unless someone goes to help her; but if anyone attempts to go near the cowshed they will break every bone in his body."

Don Camillo went and clung to the altar rails. "Lord," he said to the crucified Lord, "You must hold on to me or I shall make the march on Rome!"

"Steady, Don Camillo," replied the Lord gently. "Nothing is ever gained by violence. You must try to calm these people so that they will hear reason, and avoid exasperating them to acts of violence."

"Very true," sighed Don Camillo. "One must

make them listen to reason. All the same, it seems a pity that while one is preaching reason the cows should die.''

The Lord smiled. ''If, by the use of violence, we succeed in saving a hundred beasts and kill one man and if, on the other hand, by using persuasion we lose the beasts, but avoid the loss of that man, which seems to you preferable: violence or persuasion?''

Don Camillo, who, being filled with indignation, was loath to renounce his idea of a march on Rome, shook his head. ''Lord, You are confusing the issue: this is not only a question of the loss of a hundred beasts, but also of the public patrimony; and the death of those beasts is not simply a personal disaster for Pasotti: it is also a loss for every one of us, good and bad. And it may also easily have repercussions such as may further exacerbate existing differences and create a conflict in which not only one man may die, but twenty.''

The Lord was not of his opinion. ''But if, by reasoning, you avoid one man being killed to-day, couldn't you also, by reasoning, avoid others being killed to-morrow? Don Camillo, have you lost your faith?''

Don Camillo went out for a walk across the fields because he was restless, and so it happened that quite by chance his ears began to be assailed more and more painfully by the lowing of the hundred cows at La Grande. Then he heard the voices of the men on picket duty at the barricades, and at the end of ten minutes he found himself crawling inside and along the great cement irrigation pipe that passed underneath the wire-netting at the boundaries of La Grande, and which was fortunately not in use at the moment.

"And now," thought Don Camillo, "it only remains for me to find someone waiting at the end of this pipe to knock me on the head." But there was nobody there and Don Camillo was left in peace to make his way cautiously along the entire length of the pipe in the direction of the farm.

"Halt!" said a voice presently, and Don Camillo made one leap out of the end of his pipe to shelter behind a tree-trunk.

"Halt or I fire!" repeated the voice, which came from behind another tree-trunk on the farther side of the pipe.

It was an evening of coincidences, and Don Camillo, quite by chance, found himself grasping an appliance made of steel. He manipulated a certain movable gadget and replied:

"Be careful, Peppone, because I also shall fire."

"Ah!" muttered the other. "I might have known that I should find you mixed up in this business."

"Truce of God," said Don Camillo; "and if either of us breaks it he is damned. I am now going to count and when I say 'three' we both jump into that ditch."

"You wouldn't be a priest if you weren't so mistrustful," replied Peppone, and at the count of three he jumped and they found themselves sitting together at the bottom of the ditch.

From the cowshed came the desperate lowing of the cows, and it was enough to make one sweat with anguish. "I suppose you enjoy such music," muttered Don Camillo. "A pity that it will stop when all the cows have died. You're a fine fellow to hold on, aren't you? Why not persuade the labourers to burn the crops and also the barns that contain them? Just think now of poor Pasotti's fury if he were driven to take refuge in some Swiss hotel and to spend those few millions that he has deposited over there."

"He would have to reach Switzerland first!" growled Peppone threateningly.

"Exactly!" exclaimed Don Camillo. "It's about time we did away with that old Fifth Commandment which forbids us to kill! And when one comes eventually face to face with Almighty God one will only have to speak out bluntly: 'That's quite enough from You, my dear Eternal Father, or Peppone will proclaim a general strike and make everyone fold their arms!' By the way, Peppone, how are you going to get the cherubim to fold their arms? Have you thought of that?"

Peppone's roar vied with that of the expecting cow, whose complaints were heartrending. "You are no priest!" he vociferated. "You are the chief of the *Ghepeù!*"

"The *Gestapo,*" Don Camillo corrected him. "The *Ghepeù* is your affair."

"You go about by night, in other people's houses, clutching a tommy-gun like a bandit!"

"And what about you?" inquired Don Camillo mildly.

"I am in the service of the people!"

"And I am in God's service!"

Peppone kicked a stone. "No use trying to argue

with a priest! Before you have uttered two words they have dragged in politics!"

"Peppone," began Don Camillo gently, but the other cut him short:

"Now don't you begin jawing about the national patrimony and rubbish of that kind or as there is a God above I shall shoot you!" he exclaimed.

Don Camillo shook his head. "No use trying to argue with a Red. Before you have uttered two words they drag in politics!"

The cow that was about to calve complained loudly.

"Who goes there?" came a sudden voice from someone very close to the ditch. Then Brusco, Il Magro and Il Bigio made their appearance.

"Go and take a walk along the road to the mill," Peppone ordered them.

"All right," replied Brusco; "but who are you talking to?"

"To your damned soul," roared Peppone furiously.

"That cow that is going to calve is fairly bellowing," muttered Brusco.

"Go and tell the priest about it!" bawled Peppone. "And let her rot! I am working for the interests of the people, not of cows!"

"Keep your hair on, chief," stammered Brusco, making off hastily with his companions.

"Very well, Peppone," whispered Don Camillo; "and now we are going to work for the interests of the people."

"What do you intend to do?"

Don Camillo set out quietly along the ditch towards the farm and Peppone told him to halt or he would get what he was asking for between the shoulders.

"Peppone is as stubborn as a mule," said Don Camillo calmly, "but he doesn't shoot at the backs of poor priests who are doing what God has commanded them to do."

Then Peppone swore blasphemously and Don Camillo turned on him in a flash. "If you don't stop behaving like a balky horse, I shall give you one on the jaw, exactly as I did to your celebrated federal champion. . . ."

"You needn't tell me: I knew all along that it could only be you. But that was quite another matter."

Don Camillo walked along quietly, followed by

the other muttering and threatening to shoot. As they approached the cowshed another voice called to them to halt.

"Go to hell!" replied Peppone. "I am here myself now, so you can get along to the dairy."

Don Camillo did not even vouchsafe a glance at the cowshed door with its seals. He went straight up the stairs to the hay-loft above it and called in a low voice: "Giacomo."

The old cowman who had come to see him earlier and had related the story of the cow rose out of the hay. Don Camillo produced an electric torch and, shifting a bale of hay, revealed a trap-door.

"Go down," said Don Camillo to the old man, who climbed down and disappeared for a considerable time.

"She's had her calf all right," he whispered when he returned. "I've seen a thousand of them through it and I know more than any vet."

"Now go along home," Don Camillo told the old man, and the old man went.

Then Don Camillo opened the trap-door again and sent a bale of hay through the opening.

"What do you think you are doing?" asked Peppone, who had so far remained hidden.

"Help me to throw down these bales and then I'll tell you."

Grumbling as he did so, Peppone set to work chucking down the bales, and when Don Camillo had let himself down after them into the cowshed, Peppone followed him.

Don Camillo carried a bale to a right-hand manger and broke its lashings. "You'd better attend to the left-hand mangers," he said to Peppone.

"Not if you murder me!" shouted Peppone, seizing a bale and carrying it to the manger.

They worked like an army of oxen. Then there was the business of making the beasts drink and, since they were dealing with a modern cowshed with its drinking-troughs placed along its outer walls, it was a matter of making one hundred cows right-about-turn and then belabouring their horns to stop them from drinking themselves to death.

When all was finished it was still dark in the cowshed, but that was merely because all the shutters of the windows had been sealed from the outside.

"It's three o'clock in the afternoon," said Don Camillo, peering at his watch. "We shall have to wait until evening before we can get out!"

179

Peppone was biting his own fists with fury, but there was nothing for it but patience. When evening fell, Peppone and Don Camillo were still playing cards by the light of an oil lamp.

"I'm so hungry I could swallow a bishop whole!" exclaimed Peppone savagely.

"Hard on the digestion, Mr. Mayor," replied Don Camillo quietly, though he himself was faint with hunger and could have devoured a cardinal. "Before saying you are hungry, you should wait until you have fasted for as many days as these beasts."

Before leaving they again filled all the mangers with hay. Peppone tried to resist, saying that it was betraying the people, but Don Camillo was inflexible.

And so it happened that during the night there was a deathly silence in the cowshed, and old Pasotti, hearing no more lowing from the cows, became afraid that they must be so far gone that they had not even the strength to complain. In the morning he made a move to treat with Peppone, and with a little give and take on both sides the strike was settled and things resumed their normal course.

In the afternoon Peppone turned up at the presbytery.

"Well," said Don Camillo in honeyed tones, "you revolutionaries should always listen to advice from your old parish priest. You really should, my dear children."

Peppone stood with folded arms, struck speechless by such shameless audacity. Then he blurted out: "But my tommy-gun, *reverendo!*"

"Your tommy-gun?" replied Don Camillo with a smile. "I'm afraid I don't understand. You had it yourself."

"Yes, I did have it when we were leaving the cowshed, but then you took advantage of my exhaustion and stole it from me."

"Now that you mention it, I believe you're right," replied Don Camillo with disarming candour. "You must forgive me, Peppone, but the truth is that I am getting old and I don't seem able to remember where I've put it."

"*Reverendo!*" exclaimed Peppone indignantly. "But that's the second you've filched from me!"

"Never mind, my son. Don't worry. You will easily find another. Who knows how many you have even now lying about your house!"

"You are one of those priests that, one way or another, compel a decent man to become a Mohammedan!"

"Very possibly," replied Don Camillo, "but then you, Peppone, are not a decent man."

Peppone flung his hat on the ground.

"If you were a decent man," the priest went on, "you would be thanking me for what I have done for you and for the people."

Peppone picked up his hat, jammed it on to his head and turned away. From the threshold he spoke: "You can rob me of not only two but two hundred thousand tommy-guns, but when the time comes I shall always have a .75 to train on this infernal house!"

"And I shall always find an 81 mortar with which to retaliate," replied Don Camillo calmly.

As he was passing the open door of the church and could see the altar, Peppone angrily pulled off his hat and then crammed it on again hastily lest anyone should see him.

But the Lord had already seen and when Don Camillo came into the church He said gaily: "Peppone went by just now and took off his hat to Me."

"You be careful, Lord," replied Don Camillo. "Remember there was someone before who kissed You and then sold You for thirty pieces of silver. That fellow who took off his hat had told me only three minutes earlier that when the time came he would always find a .75 with which to fire upon the house of God!"

"And what did you reply?"

"That I would always manage to find an 81 mortar with which to fire on his headquarters."

"I understand, Don Camillo. But the trouble is that you are already in possession of that mortar."

Don Camillo spread out his arms. "Lord," he said, "there are so many odds and ends that a man hesitates to throw away because of associations. We are all of us a bit sentimental. And then, in any case, isn't it better that such a thing should be in my house than in someone else's?"

"Don Camillo is always in the right," smiled the Lord, "just as long as he plays fair."

"No fear about that; I have the best Adviser in the universe," replied Don Camillo, and to this the Lord could make no reply.

THE PROCESSION

EVERY YEAR, at the time of the blessing of the village, the crucified Lord from above the altar was carried in procession as far as the river bank, where the river also was blessed in order that it should refrain from excesses and behave decently.

Once again it seemed as though everything would take place with the customary regularity, and Don Camillo was thinking over the final touches to be given to the programme of the celebrations when Brusco made his appearance at the presbytery.

"The secretary of our local section," said Brusco, "sends me to inform you that the entire section will take part in the procession complete with all its banners."

"Convey my thanks to Secretary Peppone," replied Don Camillo. "I shall be only too happy for all the men of the section to be present. But they must be good enough to leave their banners at home. Political banners have no place in religious processions and must not appear in them. Those are the orders that I have received."

Brusco retired, and very soon Peppone arrived, red in the face and with his eyes popping out of his head.

"We are just as much Christians as all the rest of them!" he shouted, bursting into the presbytery without even knocking on the door. "In what way are we different from other folk?"

"In not taking off your hats when you come into other people's houses," said Don Camillo quietly.

Peppone snatched his hat from his head.

"Now you are just like any other Christian," said Don Camillo.

"Then why can't we join the procession with our flag?" shouted Peppone. "Is it the flag of thieves and murderers?"

"No, Comrade Peppone," Don Camillo explained, lighting his cigar. "But the flag of a party cannot be admitted. This procession is concerned with religion and not with politics."

"Then the flags of Catholic Action should also be excluded!"

"And why? Catholic Action is not a political party, as may be judged from the fact that I am its local secretary. Indeed, I strongly advise you and your comrades to join it."

Peppone sniggered. "If you want to save your black soul, you had better join our Party!"

Don Camillo raised his arms. "Supposing we leave it at that," he replied, smiling. "We all stay as we are and remain friends."

"You and I have never been friends," Peppone asserted.

"Not even when we were in the mountains together?"

"No! That was merely a strategic alliance. For the triumph of our arms, it is allowable to make an alliance even with priests."

"Very well," said Don Camillo calmly. "Nevertheless, if you want to join in the procession you must leave your flag at home."

Peppone ground his teeth. "If you think you can play at being Duce, *reverendo*, you're making a big mistake!" he exclaimed. "Either our flag marches or there won't be any procession!"

Don Camillo was not impressed. "He'll get over it," he said to himself. And in fact, during the three days preceding the Sunday of the blessing, nothing more was said about the argument. But on the Sunday, an hour before Mass, scared people began to arrive at the presbytery. Early that morning Peppone's satellites had called at every house in the village to warn the inmates that anyone who ventured to take part in the procession would do so at the risk of life and limb.

"No one has said anything of the kind to me," replied Don Camillo. "I am therefore not interested."

The procession was to take place immediately after Mass, and while Don Camillo was vesting for it in the sacristy he was interrupted by a group of parishioners.

"What are we going to do?" they asked him.

"We are going in procession," replied Don Camillo quietly.

"But those ruffians are quite capable of throwing

bombs at it," they objected. "You cannot expose your parishioners to such a risk. In our opinion, you ought to postpone the procession, give notice to the public authorities of the town, and have the procession as soon as there are sufficient police on the spot to protect the people."

"I see," remarked Don Camillo. "And in the meantime we might explain to the martyrs of our faith that they made a big mistake in behaving as they did and that, instead of going off to spread Christianity when it was forbidden, they should have waited quietly until they had police to protect them."

Then Don Camillo showed his visitors the way to the door, and they went off, muttering and grumbling.

Shortly afterwards a number of aged men and women entered the church. "We are coming along, Don Camillo," they said.

"You are going straight back to your houses!" replied Don Camillo. "God will take note of your pious intentions, but this is decidedly one of those occasions when old men, old women and children should remain at home."

A number of people had lingered in front of the

church, but when the sound of firing was heard in the distance (occasioned by Brusco letting off a tommy-gun into the air as a demonstration), even the group of survivors melted away, and Don Camillo, appearing upon the threshold of the sacristy, found the square as bare as a billiard table.

"Are we going now, Don Camillo?" inquired the Lord from above the altar. "The river must be looking beautiful in this sunshine and I shall really enjoy seeing it."

"We are going all right," replied Don Camillo. "But I am afraid that this time I shall be the entire procession. If You can put up with that . . ."

"Where there is Don Camillo, he is sufficient in himself," said the Lord, smiling.

Don Camillo hastily put on the leather harness with the support for the foot of the Cross, lifted the enormous crucifix from the altar and adjusted it in the socket. Then he sighed: "All the same, they need not have made this cross quite so heavy."

"You're telling Me!" replied the Lord, smiling. "Didn't I carry it to the top of the hill, and I never had shoulders such as yours?"

A few moments later Don Camillo, bearing his enormous crucifix, emerged solemnly from the door of the church.

The village was completely deserted; people were cowering in their houses and watching through the cracks of the shutters.

"I must look like one of those friars who used to carry a big black cross through villages smitten by the plague," said Don Camillo to himself. Then he began a psalm in his ringing baritone, which seemed to acquire volume in the silence.

Having crossed the square, he began to walk down the main street, and here again there was emptiness and silence. A small dog came out of a side street and began quietly to follow Don Camillo.

"Get out!" muttered Don Camillo.

"Let it alone," whispered the Lord from His Cross; "and then Peppone won't be able to say that not even a dog walked in the procession."

The street curved at its end and then came the lane that led to the river bank. Don Camillo had no sooner turned the bend when he found the way unexpectedly obstructed. Two hundred men had collected and stood silently across it with straddled legs and folded arms. In front of them stood Peppone, his hands on his hips.

Don Camillo wished he were a tank. But since he could only be Don Camillo, he advanced until he was within a yard of Peppone and then halted. Then he lifted the enormous crucifix from its socket and raised it in his hands, brandishing it as though it were a club.

"Lord," said Don Camillo, "hold on tight; I am going to strike!"

But there was no need, because, having in a flash grasped the situation, the men withdrew to the sides of the road, and as though by enchantment the way lay open before him.

Only Peppone, his arms akimbo and his legs wide apart, remained standing in the middle of the road. Don Camillo replaced the crucifix in its socket and marched straight at him, and Peppone moved to one side.

"I'm not shifting myself for your sake, but for His," said Peppone, pointing to the crucifix.

"Then take that hat off your head!" replied Don Camillo, without so much as looking at him.

Peppone pulled off his hat and Don Camillo

marched solemnly through two rows of Peppone's men.

When he reached the river bank he stopped. "Lord," said Don Camillo in a loud voice, "if the few decent people in this filthy village could build themselves a Noah's Ark and float safely upon the waters, I would ask You to send such a flood as would break down this bank and submerge the whole countryside. But as these few decent folk live in brick houses exactly similar to those of their rotten neighbours, and as it would not be just that the good should suffer for the sins of scoundrels such as the Mayor Peppone and his gang of godless brigands, I ask You to save this countryside from the waters and to give it every prosperity."

"Amen," came Peppone's voice from just behind him.

"Amen," came the response from behind Peppone of all the men who had followed the crucifix.

Don Camillo set out on the return journey, and when he reached the threshold of the church and turned round so that the Lord might bestow a final blessing upon the distant river, he found standing before him: the small dog, Peppone,

Peppone's men and every inhabitant of the village, not excluding the chemist, who was an atheist, but who felt that never in his life had he dreamed of a priest such as Don Camillo who could make even the Eternal Father quite tolerable.

THE MEETING

As soon as Peppone read a notice pasted up at the street corners to the effect that a stranger from the town had been invited by the local section of the Liberal Party to hold a meeting in the square, he leaped into the air.

"Here, in the Red stronghold! Are we to tolerate such a provocation?" he bawled. "We shall very soon see who commands here!"

Then he summoned his general staff and the stupendous occurrence was studied and analysed. The proposal to set fire immediately to the headquarters of the Liberal Party was rejected. That of forbidding the meeting met with the same fate.

"There you have democracy!" said Peppone sententiously. "When an unknown scoundrel can permit himself the luxury of speaking in a public square!"

They decided to remain within the bounds of law and order: general mobilization of all their members, organization of squads to supervise things generally and avoid any ambush, occupation of strategic points and protection of their own headquarters. Pickets were to stand by to summon reinforcements from neighbouring sectors.

"The fact that they are holding a public meeting here shows that they are confident of overpowering us," said Peppone. "But in any case they will not find us unprepared."

Scouts placed along the roads leading to the village were to report any suspicious movement, and were already on duty from early Saturday morning, but they failed to sight so much as a cat throughout the entire day. During the night Smilzo discovered a questionable cyclist, but he proved to be only a normal drunk. The meeting was to take place in the course of Sunday afternoon, and up to three o'clock not a soul had put in an appearance.

"They will be coming by the three-fifty-five train," said Peppone. And he placed a large contingent of his men in and around the railway station.

The train steamed in and the only person who got out was a thin little man carrying a small fibre suitcase.

"It's obvious that they got wind of something and didn't feel strong enough to meet the emergency," said Peppone.

At that moment the little man came up to him and, taking off his hat, politely inquired whether Peppone would be so kind as to direct him to the headquarters of the Liberal Party.

Peppone stared at him in amazement. "The headquarters of the Liberal Party?"

"Yes," explained the little man. "I am due to make a short speech in twenty minutes' time, and I should not like to be late."

Everybody was looking at Peppone, and Peppone scratched his head. "It is really rather difficult to explain, because the centre of the village is over a mile away."

The little man made a gesture of anxiety. "Will it be possible for me to find some means of transport?"

"I have a lorry outside," muttered Peppone, "if you care to come along."

The little man thanked him. Then, when they

got outside and he saw the lorry full of surly faces, red handkerchiefs and Communist badges, he looked at Peppone.

"I am their leader," said Peppone. "Get up in front with me."

Half-way to the village Peppone stopped the engine and examined his passenger, who was a middle-aged gentleman, very thin and with clear-cut features.

"So you are a Liberal?"

"I am," replied the gentleman.

"And you are not alarmed at finding yourself alone here among fifty Communists?"

"No," replied the man quietly. A threatening murmur came from the men in the lorry.

"What have you got in that suitcase?"

The man began to laugh and opened the case. "Pyjamas, a pair of slippers and a tooth-brush," he exclaimed.

Peppone pushed his hat on to the back of his head and slapped his thigh. "You must be crazy!" he bellowed. "And may one be allowed to inquire why you aren't afraid?"

"Simply because I am alone and there are fifty of you," the little man explained quietly.

"What the hell has that got to do with it?" howled Peppone. "Doesn't it strike you that I could pick you up with one hand and throw you into that ditch?"

"No; it doesn't strike me," replied the little man as quietly as before.

"Then you really must either be crazy or irresponsible, or deliberately out to gull us."

The little man laughed again. "It is much simpler than that," he said. "I am just an ordinary, decent man."

"Ah, no, my good sir!" exclaimed Peppone, leaping to his feet. "If you were an ordinary, decent man, you wouldn't be an enemy of the people! A slave of reaction! An instrument of capitalism!"

"I am nobody's enemy and nobody's slave. I am merely a man who thinks differently from you."

Peppone started the engine and the lorry dashed forward. "I suppose you made your will before coming here?" he jeered as he jammed his foot on the accelerator.

"No," replied the little man, unperturbed. "All I have is my work, and if I should die I couldn't leave it to anyone else."

Before entering the village Peppone pulled up for a moment to speak to Smilzo, who was acting as orderly with his motor-bike. Then, by way of several side streets, they reached the headquarters of the Liberal Party. Doors and windows were closed.

"Nobody here," said Peppone gloomily.

"They must all be in the square, of course. It is already late," retorted the little man.

"I suppose that's it," replied Peppone, winking at Brusco.

When they reached the square Peppone and his men got out of the lorry and surrounded the little man and thrust a way through the crowd to the platform. The little man climbed on to it and found himself face to face with two thousand men, all wearing the red handkerchief.

The little man turned to Peppone, who had followed him on to the platform. "Excuse me," he inquired, "but have I by any chance come to the wrong meeting?"

"No," Peppone reassured him. "The fact is that there are only twenty-three Liberals in the whole district, and they don't show up much in a crowd. To tell you the truth, if I had been in your place, it would never have entered my head to hold a meeting here."

"It seems obvious that the Liberals have more confidence in the democratic discipline of the Communists than you have," replied the little man.

Peppone looked disconcerted for a moment, then he went up to the microphone. "Comrades," he shouted, "I wish to introduce to you this gentleman who will make you a speech that will send you all off to join the Liberal Party."

A roar of laughter greeted this sally, and as soon as it died the little man began speaking. "I want to thank your leader for his courtesy," he said, "but it is my duty to explain to you that his statement does not tally with my wishes. Because if, at the end of my speech, you all went to join the Liberal Party, I should feel it incumbent upon me to go and join the Communist Party, and that would be against all my principles."

He was unable to continue, because just at that moment a tomato whistled through the air and struck him in the face.

The crowd began jeering and Peppone went white. "Anyone who laughs is a swine!" he

shouted into the microphone, and there was immediate silence.

The little man had not moved, and was trying
to clean his face with his hand. Peppone was a
child of instinct, and quite unconsciously was
capable of magnificent impulses; he pulled his
handkerchief from his pocket, then he put it back
again and unknotted the vast red handkerchief
from his neck and offered it to the little man. "I
wore it in the mountains," he said. "Wipe your
face."

"Bravo, Peppone!" thundered a voice from the
first-floor window of a neighbouring house.

"I don't need the approval of the clergy," replied
Peppone arrogantly, while Don Camillo bit his
tongue with fury at having let his feelings get the
better of him.

The little man shook his head, bowed and approached the microphone. "There is too much
history attached to that handkerchief for me to soil
it with the traces of a vulgar episode that belongs to
the less heroic chronicles of our times," he said. "A
handkerchief such as we use for a common cold
suffices for such a purpose."

Peppone flushed scarlet and also bowed, and then

a wave of emotion swept the crowd and there was vigorous applause while the hooligan lad who had thrown the tomato was kicked off the square.

The little man resumed his speech calmly. He was quiet, without any trace of bitterness, smoothing off corners, avoiding contentious arguments, being fully aware that should he let himself go, he could do so with impunity and would therefore be guilty of taking a cowardly advantage of the situation. At the end, he was applauded, and when he stepped down from the platform a way was cleared before him.

When he reached the far end of the square and found himself beneath the portico of the town hall he stood helplessly with his suitcase in his hand, not knowing where to go or what to do.

At that moment Don Camillo hurried up and turned to Peppone, who was standing just behind the little man. "You've lost no time, have you, you godless rascal, in making up to this Liberal priest-eater."

"What?" gasped Peppone, also turning towards the little man. "Then you are a priest-eater?"

"But . . ." stammered the little man.

"Hold your tongue," Don Camillo interrupted

him. "You ought to be ashamed, you who demand a free Church in a free State!"

The little man attempted to protest, but Peppone cut him short before he could utter a word. "Bravo!" he bawled. "Give me your hand! When a man is a priest-eater he is my friend, even if he is a Liberal reactionary!"

"Hurrah!" shouted Peppone's satellites.

"You are my guest!" said Peppone to the little man.

"Nothing of the kind," retorted Don Camillo. "This gentleman is my guest. I am not a boor who fires tomatoes at his adversaries!"

Peppone pushed himself menacingly in front of Don Camillo. "I have said that he is my guest," he repeated fiercely.

"And as I have said the same thing," replied Don Camillo, "it means that if you want to come to blows with me about it, you can also have those that are due to your ruffianly Dynamos!"

Peppone clutched his fists.

"Come away," said Brusco. "In another minute you'll be at fisticuffs with the priest in the public square!"

In the end, the matter was settled in favour of a

meeting on neutral territory. All three of them went out into the country to luncheon with Gigiotto, a host completely indifferent to politics, and thus even the democratic encounter led to no results of any kind.

ON THE RIVER BANK

BETWEEN ONE and three o'clock of the afternoon in the month of August, the heat in these districts that lie under hemp and buckwheat is something that can be both seen and felt. It is almost as though a great curtain of boiling glass hung at a few inches from one's nose. If you are crossing a bridge and you look down into the canal, its bed is dry and cracked with here and there a dead fish, and when from the road along the river bank you look at a cemetery you almost seem to hear the bones rattling beneath the boiling sun.

Along the main road you will meet an occasional wagon piled high with sand, with the driver sound asleep lying face downwards on top of his load, his stomach cool and his spine incandescent, or sitting on the shaft fishing out pieces from half a water-melon that he holds on his knees like a bowl. Then when you come to the big bank, there lies the great river, deserted, motionless and silent, and it seems not so much a river as a cemetery of dead waters.

Don Camillo was walking in the direction of the big river, with a large white handkerchief inserted between his head and his hat. It was half-past one of an August afternoon and, seeing him thus, alone upon the white road under the burning rays of the sun, it was not possible to imagine anything blacker or more blatantly priest-like.

"If there is at this moment anyone within a radius of twenty miles who is not asleep, I'll eat my hat," said Don Camillo to himself. Then he climbed over the bank and sat down in the shade of a thicket of acacias and watched the water shining through the interstices of the foliage. Presently he took off his clothes, folding each garment carefully and rolling them all into a bundle that he hid among the bushes, and wearing only his drawers, went and flung himself into the water.

Everything was perfectly quiet; no one could

possibly have seen him, because, in addition to selecting the hour of siesta, he had also chosen the most secluded spot. In any case, he was prudent, and at the end of half an hour he climbed out of the water among the acacias and reached the bush where he had hidden his clothes, only to discover that the clothes were no longer there.

Don Camillo felt his breath fail him.

There could be no question of theft: nobody could possibly covet an old and faded cassock. It must mean that some devilry was afoot. And in fact at that very moment he heard voices approaching from the top of the bank. As soon as Don Camillo was able to see something he made out a crowd of young men and girls, and then he recognized Smilzo as their leader and was seized with an almost uncontrollable desire to break a branch from the acacias and use it on their backs.

But he fully realized that he would only be gratifying his adversaries: what they were playing for was to enjoy the spectacle of Don Camillo in his drawers. So he dived back into the water and, swimming beneath the surface, reached a little island in the middle of the river. Creeping ashore, he disappeared among the reeds.

But although his enemies had been unable to see him land they had become aware of his retreat and had now flung themselves down along the bank and lay waiting for him, laughing and singing.

Don Camillo was in a state of siege.

How weak is a strong man when he feels himself to be ridiculous! Don Camillo lay among the reeds and waited. Lying there unseen and yet able to see, he beheld the arrival of Peppone followed by Brusco, Bigio and his entire staff. Smilzo explained the situation with many gestures and there was much laughter. Then came more people, and Don Camillo realized that the Reds were out to make him pay dearly for all past and present accounts and that they had hit upon the best of all systems because, when anyone has made himself ridiculous, nobody is ever afraid of him again, not even if his fists weigh a ton and he represents the Eternal Father. And in any case it was all grossly unfair because Don Camillo had never wished to frighten anyone except the devil. But somehow politics had contrived so to distort facts that the Reds had come to consider the parish priest as their enemy and to say that if things were not as they wished it was all the fault of the priests. When things go wrong it always seems less important to seek a remedy than to find a scapegoat.

"Lord," said Don Camillo, "I am ashamed to address You in my drawers, but the matter is becoming serious and if it is not a mortal sin for a poor parish priest who is dying of the heat to go bathing, please help me, because I am quite unable to help myself."

The watchers had brought flasks of wine, parcels of food and an accordion. The river bank had been transformed into a beach and it was obvious that they had not the faintest intention of raising the siege. Indeed, they had extended it to beyond the celebrated locality of the ford, two hundred yards of shore consisting of shrubs and undergrowth. Not a soul had set foot in this area since 1945, because the retreating Germans had destroyed all the bridges and mined both banks at the ford. After a couple of disastrous attempts, the mine-removal squads had merely isolated the area with posts and barbed wire.

There were none of Peppone's men in that region: they were unnecessary, as no one but a lunatic would think of going near the minefield. There was thus nothing to be done, because should he attempt to land beyond the watchers downstream, Don Camillo would find himself in the middle of the village, and any attempt to get ashore upstream would lead him into the minefield. A priest wearing only his drawers could not permit himself such luxuries.

Don Camillo did not move: he remained lying on the damp earth, chewing a reed and following his own train of thought. "Well," he concluded, "a respectable man remains a respectable man even in his drawers. The important thing is that he should perform some reputable action and then his clothing ceases to have any importance."

The daylight was now beginning to fail and the watchers on the bank were lighting torches and lanterns. As soon as the green of the grass became black, Don Camillo let himself down into the water and made his way cautiously upstream until his feet touched bottom at the ford. Then he struck out for the bank. No one could see him, as he was walking rather than swimming, only lifting his mouth out of the water at intervals to get his breath.

Here was the shore. The difficulty was to leave the water without being seen; once among the bushes, he could easily reach the bank and by running along it duck under the rows of vines and through the buckwheat and so gain his own garden.

He grasped a bush and raised himself slowly, but just as he had almost achieved his end, the bush came up by the roots and Don Camillo fell back into the water. The splash was heard and people came running. But in a flash Don Camillo had leaped ashore and had vanished among the bushes.

There were loud cries and the entire crowd surged towards the spot just as the moon rose to give its light to the spectacle.

"Don Camillo!" bawled Peppone, thrusting his way to the front of the crowd. "Don Camillo!"

There was no reply and a deathly silence fell upon all those present.

"Don Camillo!" yelled Peppone again. "For God's sake don't move! You are in the minefield!"

"I know I am," replied the voice of Don Camillo quietly from behind a shrub in the midst of the sinister shrubbery.

Smilzo came forward carrying a bundle. "Don Camillo!" he shouted. "It was a rotten joke. Keep still and here are your clothes."

"My clothes? Oh, thank you, Smilzo. If you will be so kind as to bring them to me."

A branch was seen to move at the top of a bush some distance away. Smilzo's mouth fell open and he looked round at those behind him. The silence was broken only by an ironical laugh from Don Camillo.

Peppone seized the bundle from Smilzo's hand. "I'll bring them, Don Camillo," said Peppone, advancing slowly towards the posts and the barbed wire. He had already thrown a leg over the barrier when Smilzo sprang forward and dragged him back.

"No, chief," said Smilzo, taking the bundle from him and entering the enclosure. "He who breaks, pays."

The people shrank back; their faces were damp with sweat, and they held their hands over their mouths. Amid a leaden silence Smilzo made his way slowly towards the middle of the enclosure, placing his feet carefully.

"Here you are," said Smilzo, in the ghost of a voice, as he reached Don Camillo's bush.

"Good!" muttered Don Camillo. "And now you can come round here. You have earned the right to see Don Camillo in his drawers."

Smilzo obeyed him.

"Well? And what do you think of a parish priest in drawers?"

"I don't know," stammered Smilzo. "I've stolen trifles and I've hit a fellow now and again, but I've never really done any harm to anyone."

"*Ego te absolvo*," replied Don Camillo, making the sign of the cross on his forehead.

They walked slowly towards the bank and the crowd held its breath and waited for the explosion.

They climbed over the barbed wire and walked along the road, Don Camillo leading and Smilzo, at his heels, still walking on tiptoe as though he had not left the minefield, because he no longer knew what he was doing. Suddenly he collapsed on to the ground. Peppone, who at twenty paces' distance was leading the rest of the people, picked up Smilzo by the collar as he went by and dragged him along like a bundle of rags, without once taking his eyes from Don Camillo's back.

At the church door Don Camillo turned round for a moment, bowed politely to his parishioners and went into the church.

The others dispersed in silence and Peppone remained standing alone before the church, staring at the closed door and still clutching the collar of the unconscious Smilzo. Then he shook his head, and he also turned and went his way, still dragging his burden.

"Lord," whispered Don Camillo to the crucified Lord, "one must serve the Church, even by protecting the dignity of a parish priest in his drawers."

There was no reply.

"Lord," whispered Don Camillo anxiously, "did I really commit a mortal sin in going to bathe?"

"No," replied the Lord; "but you did commit a mortal sin when you dared Smilzo to bring you your clothes."

"I never thought he would do it. I was thoughtless, but not deliberately wicked."

From the direction of the river came the sound of a distant explosion.

"Every now and then a hare runs through the minefield, and then . . ." Don Camillo explained in an almost inaudible voice. "So we must conclude that You . . ."

"You must conclude nothing at all, Don Camillo," the Lord interrupted him, with a smile. "With the temperature you are running at this

214

moment your conclusions would scarcely be of any value."

Meanwhile, Peppone had reached the door of Smilzo's home. He knocked, and the door was opened by an old man who made no comment as Peppone handed over his burden. And it was at that moment that Peppone also heard the explosion, shook his head and remembered many things. Then he took Smilzo back from the old man for a moment and boxed his ears until his hair stood on end.

"Forward!" murmured Smilzo in a far-away voice as the old man once more took charge of him.

RAW MATERIAL

ONE AFTERNOON Don Camillo, who for a week past had been in a chronic state of agitation and had done nothing but rush to and fro, was returning from a visit to a neighbouring village. As soon as he reached his own parish he was compelled to alight from his bicycle because some men had appeared since his departure and were digging a ditch right across the road.

"We are putting in a new drain," a workman explained, "by the mayor's orders."

Then Don Camillo went straight to the town hall, and when he found Peppone he lost his temper.

"Are we all going off our heads?" he exclaimed. "Here you are, digging this filthy ditch, and don't you know that this is Friday?"

"Well!" replied Peppone, with every appearance of astonishment. "And is it forbidden to dig a ditch on a Friday?"

Don Camillo roared: "But have you realized that we are within less than two days of Sunday?"

Peppone looked worried. He rang a bell, and it was answered by Bigio. "Listen, Bigio," said Peppone. "The *reverendo* says that since to-day is Friday, it lacks less than two days to Sunday. What do you think about it?"

Bigio appeared to reflect very gravely. Then he pulled out a pencil and made calculations on a piece of paper. "Why," he said presently, "taking into consideration that it is now four o'clock in the afternoon and therefore within eight hours of midnight, it will actually be Sunday within thirty-two hours from the present time."

Don Camillo had watched all these manœuvres and was by now almost foaming at the mouth. "I understand!" he shouted. "This is all a put-up job in order to boycott the bishop's visit."

"*Reverendo*," replied Peppone, "where is the connection between our local sewage and the bishop's visit? And also, may I ask what bishop you are speaking of and why he should be coming here?"

"To the devil with your black soul!" bawled Don Camillo. "That ditch must be filled in at once, or else the bishop will be unable to pass on Sunday!"

Peppone's face looked completely blank. "Unable to pass? But then how did you pass? There are a couple of planks across the ditch, if I am not mistaken."

"But the bishop is coming by car," exclaimed Don Camillo. "We can't ask a bishop to get out of his car and walk!"

"You must forgive me. I didn't know that bishops were unable to walk," retorted Peppone. "If that is so, then it is quite another matter. Brusco, call up the town and tell them to send us a crane immediately. We'll put it near the ditch, and as soon as the bishop's car arrives the crane can grapple on to it and lift it over the ditch without the bishop having to leave it. Have you understood?"

"Perfectly, chief. And what colour crane shall I ask for?"

"Tell them chromium or nickel-plated; it will look better."

In such circumstances even a man who lacked Don Camillo's armour-plated fists might have been tempted to come to blows. But it was precisely in such cases as these that Don Camillo, on the contrary, became entirely composed. His argument was as follows: "If this fellow sets out so blatantly and deliberately to provoke me it is because he hopes that I shall lose my temper. Therefore, if I give him one on the jaw I am simply playing his game. As a fact, I should not be striking Peppone, but a mayor in the exercise of his functions, and that would make an infernal scandal and create an atmosphere not only hostile to me personally, but also to the bishop."

"Never mind," he said quietly. "Even bishops can walk."

Speaking in church that evening, he literally implored all his congregation to remain calm and to concentrate upon asking God to shed light upon the mind of their mayor in order that he might not attempt to ruin the impending ceremony, breaking up the procession and compelling the faithful to pass one at a time over a couple of insecure boards. And they must also pray God to prevent this improvised bridge from breaking under the undue strain and thus turning a day of rejoicing into one of mourning.

This diabolical address had its calculated effect upon all the women of the congregation, who, on leaving the church, collected in front of Peppone's house and carried on to such effect that at last Peppone came to a window and shouted that they could all go to hell and that the ditch would be filled in.

And so all was well, but on Sunday morning the village streets were adorned with large printed posters:

"Comrades!

"Alleging as a pretext of offence the initiation of work of public utility, the reactionaries have staged an unseemly agitation that has offended our democratic instincts. On Sunday our borough is to receive a visit from the representative of a foreign power, the same in fact who has been, indirectly, the cause of the aforementioned agitation. Bearing in mind your just resentment and indignation, we are anxious to avoid, on Sunday, any demonstration which might complicate our relations with strangers. We therefore categorically exhort you to keep your reception of this representative of a foreign power within the limits of a dignified indifference.

"Hurrah for the Democratic Republic! Hurrah for the Proletariat! Hurrah for Russia!"

This exhibition was further enlivened by a throng of Reds, who, it was easy to understand, had been specially mobilized with orders to parade the streets with *"dignified indifference"*, wearing red handkerchiefs or red ties.

Don Camillo, very white about the gills, went for a moment into the church, and was about to hurry away when he heard the Lord calling him. "Don Camillo, why are you in such a hurry?"

"I have to go and receive the bishop along the road," Don Camillo explained. "It is some distance, and then there are so many people about wearing red handkerchiefs that if the bishop does not see me immediately he will think that he has come to Stalingrad."

"And are these wearers of red handkerchiefs foreigners or of another religion?" asked the Lord.

"No; they are the usual rascals that You see before You from time to time, here in the church."

"Then if that is the case, Don Camillo, it would be better for you to take off that affair that you have strapped on under your cassock and to put it back in the cupboard."

Don Camillo removed the tommy-gun and went to put it away in the sacristy.

"You can leave it there until I tell you to take it out again," commanded the Lord, and Don Camillo shrugged his shoulders.

"If I am to wait until You tell me to use a tommy-gun, we shall be in the soup!" he exclaimed. "You aren't likely ever to give the word, and I must confess that in many instances the Old Testament . . ."

"Reactionary!" smiled the Lord. "And while you are wasting time in chattering, your poor old defenceless bishop is the prey of savage Russian Reds!"

This was a fact: the poor old defenceless bishop was indeed in the hands of the Red agitators. From as early as seven o'clock in the morning, the faithful had flocked to both sides of the main road, forming two long and impressive walls of enthusiasm, but a few minutes before the bishop's car was sighted Peppone, warned by a rocket fired by his outpost to signal the passing by of the enemy, gave the order to advance, and by a lightning manœuvre the Red forces rushed forward half a mile, so that upon his arrival the bishop found the entire road a mass of men wearing red handkerchiefs. People wandered to and fro and clustered into gossiping groups, displaying a sublime indifference towards the difficulties of the bishop's driver, who was compelled to proceed at a foot's pace, clearing a passage by continuous use of his horn.

This was in fact the *"dignified indifference"* ordained by the headquarters staff. Peppone and his satellites, mingling with the crowd, were chuckling with delight.

The bishop (that celebrated and very aged man, white-haired and bent, whose voice, when he spoke, appeared to come not from his lips, but from another century) immediately understood the *"dignified indifference"* and, telling his driver to stop the car (which was an open tourist model), made an abortive movement to open the door, allowing it to seem as if he lacked the necessary strength. Brusco, who was standing nearby, fell into the trap and when he realized his mistake, because of the kick Peppone had landed on his shin, it was too late and he had already opened the door.

"Thank you, my son," said the bishop. "I think it would be better if I walked to the village."

"But it is some distance," muttered Bigio, also receiving a kick on the shin.

"Never mind," replied the bishop, laughing. "I shouldn't like to disturb your political meeting."

"It is not a political meeting," explained Peppone gloomily. "They are only workers quietly discussing their own affairs. You'd better stay in your car."

But by now the bishop was standing in the road and Brusco had earned another kick because, realizing that he was unsteady on his feet, he had offered the support of his arm.

"Thank you, thank you so much, my son," said the bishop, and he set out, having made a sign to his secretary not to accompany him, as he wished to go alone.

And it was in this manner, at the head of the entire Red horde, that he reached the zone occupied by Don Camillo's forces, and beside the bishop were Peppone, his headquarters staff and all his most devoted henchmen, because, as Peppone had very wisely pointed out, the slightest gesture of discourtesy shown by any hot-headed fool to the representative of a foreign power would have given the reactionaries the opportunity of their lives.

"The order remains and will remain unchanged," concluded Peppone. *"Dignified indifference."*

The instant he sighted the bishop Don Camillo rushed towards him. "Monsignore," he exclaimed with great agitation, "forgive me, but it was not my fault! I was awaiting you with all the faithful, but at the last moment . . ."

"Don't worry," smiled the bishop. "The fault has been entirely my own, because I took it into my head to leave the car and take a walk. All bishops, as they get old, become a little crazy!"

The faithful applauded, the bands struck up and the bishop looked about him with obvious enjoyment. "What a lovely village," he said as he walked on. "Really lovely, and so beautifully neat and clean. You must have an excellent local administration."

"We do what we can for the good of the people," replied Brusco, receiving his third kick from Peppone.

The bishop, on reaching the square, immediately noticed the fountain and halted. "A fountain in a village of the Bassa!" he exclaimed. "That must mean that you have water!"

"Only a matter of bringing it here, Eminence,"

H   225

replied Bigio, to whom belonged the chief credit of the enterprise. "We laid three hundred yards of pipes and there, with God's help, was the water."

Bigio got his kick in due time and then, as the fountain was situated opposite the People's Palace, the bishop noticed the large new edifice and was interested. "And what is that handsome building?"

"The People's Palace," replied Peppone proudly.

"But it is really magnificent!" exclaimed the bishop.

"Would you care to go over it?" said Peppone on an impulse, while a terrible kick on the shins made him wince. That particular kick had come from Don Camillo.

The bishop's secretary, a lean young man with spectacles perched upon a big nose, had hurried forward to warn him that this was an unsuitable departure from routine, but the bishop had already entered the building. And they showed him everything: the gymnasium, the reading-room, the writing-room, and when they reached the library he went up to the bookshelves and studied the titles of the books. Before the bookcase labelled "Political", which was filled with propagandist books and pamphlets, he said nothing but only sighed, and Peppone, who was close to him, noticed that sigh.

"Nobody ever reads them, Monsignore," whispered Peppone.

He spared his visitor the inspection of the offices, but could not resist the temptation to show off the tea-room, which was the object of his special pride, and thus the bishop, on his way out, was confronted by the enormous portrait of the man with the big moustache and the small eyes.

"You know how it is in politics," said Peppone in a confidential voice. "And then, you may believe me, he isn't really such a bad fellow."

"May God in His mercy shed light upon his mind also," replied the bishop quietly.

Throughout all this business Don Camillo's psychological position was peculiar. Because, while he was foaming at the mouth with indignation at the presumption upon the bishop's kindness that dared to inflict upon him an inspection of the People's Palace, which was a foundation that surely cried to God for vengeance, on the other hand he was proud that the bishop should know how progressive and up-to-date a village he had come to visit. Moreover, he was not displeased that the bishop should realize the strength of the local leftist organization, since it could only enhance the merits of his own recreation centre in the bishop's eyes.

When the inspection was at an end Don Camillo approached the bishop. "It seems a pity, Monsignore," he said, so loudly that Peppone could not fail to hear him, "it seems a pity that our mayor has not shown you the arsenal. It is believed to be the most fully supplied of the entire province."

Peppone was about to retort, but the bishop forestalled him. "Surely not so well supplied as your own," he replied, laughing.

"Well said!" exclaimed Bigio.

"He even has an S.S. mortar buried somewhere," added Brusco.

The bishop turned towards Peppone's staff. "You would insist on having him back again," he said; "and now you can keep him. Didn't I warn you that he was dangerous?"

"He doesn't manage to scare us," said Peppone, with a grin.

"Keep an eye on him, all the same," the bishop advised him.

Don Camillo shook his head. "You will always have your joke, Monsignore!" he exclaimed. "But you can have no idea what these people are like!"

On his way out the bishop passed the news-board, saw the poster and paused to read it.

"Ah," he remarked, "you are expecting a visit from the representative of a foreign power! And who may that be, Don Camillo?"

"I know very little of politics," replied Don Camillo. "We must ask the gentleman who is responsible for the poster. Mr. Mayor, Monsignore wishes to know who is the representative of a foreign power who is mentioned in your manifesto?"

"Oh," said Peppone, after a moment's hesitation, "the usual American."

"I understand," replied the bishop. "One of those Americans who are looking for oil in these parts. Am I right?"

"Yes," said Peppone. "It's a downright scandal: any oil there may be belongs to us."

"I quite agree," said the bishop with the utmost gravity. "But I think you were wise to tell your people to limit their reactions to a dignified indifference. In my view, we should be foolish to quarrel with America. Don't you agree?"

Peppone spread out his arms. "Monsignore," he said, "you know how it is: one puts up with as much as can be borne and then comes the final straw!"

When the bishop arrived in front of the church he found all the local children from Don Camillo's recreation centre mustered in a neat formation, singing a song of welcome. Then an immense bouquet of flowers was seen to detach itself from the formation, and when it came to a halt in front of the bishop the flowers moved upwards and revealed a tiny child, so lovely and with such beautiful curls and clothes that all the women present went nearly out of their minds. There was complete silence while the infant, without pause or punctuation and in a voice as clear and pure as a little spring of water, recited a poem in the bishop's honour. After which everyone present applauded the child vociferously, exclaiming that he was adorable.

Peppone went up to Don Camillo. "Dastard!" he hissed in his ear. "You have taken advantage of a child's innocence in order to make me ridiculous before everybody! I shall break every bone in your body. And as for that brat, I shall show him where he gets off. You have contaminated him, and I shall chuck him into the river!"

"Good hunting!" replied Don Camillo. "He's your own son, and you can do as you like with him."

And it really was a shocking episode, because Peppone, carrying off the poor child to the river like a bundle, compelled him after fearful threats to recite three times over the poem in honour of the bishop . . . of that poor old weak and ingenious bishop who, being the *"representative of a foreign power"* (the Vatican), had been received, according to plan, with *"dignified indifference"*.

THE BELL

DON CAMILLO, after a week during which he had attacked Bigio at least three times daily wherever he met him, shouting that he and all his breed of house-painters were highway robbers and lived only by extortion, had at last succeeded in agreeing with him on a price for whitewashing the outside walls of the presbytery. And now, from time to time, he went to sit for a while upon the bench in the church square so that he might enjoy the spectacle of those gleaming white walls that, together with the newly painted shutters and the climbing jasmine over the doorway, made a really beautiful effect.

But after each gratifying contemplation, Don

Camillo turned to look at the church tower and sighed heavily, thinking of Geltrude. Geltrude had been carried off by the Germans, and Don Camillo had therefore now been fretting for her for nearly three years. For Geltrude had been the largest of the church bells, and only God could provide the necessary cash for the purchase of another bell of her lordly proportions.

"Stop brooding, Don Camillo," said the Lord above the altar one day. "A parish can get along very nicely even if the church tower lacks one of its bells. In such a matter, noise is not everything. God has very sharp ears and can hear perfectly well even if He is called by a bell the size of a hazel nut."

"Of course He can," replied Don Camillo with a sigh. "But men are hard of hearing, and it is chiefly to call them that bells are needed: the masses do listen to those who make the loudest noise."

"Well, Don Camillo, peg away and you'll succeed."

"But, Lord, I have tried everything. Those who would like to give haven't the money, and the rich won't shell out even if you put a knife to their throats. I've been very near success a couple of times with the football pools. . . . A pity! If only someone had given me the shadow of a tip—just one name and I could have bought a dozen bells. . . ."

The Lord smiled. "You must forgive My carelessness, Don Camillo. You want Me in the coming year to keep My mind on the football championship? Are you also interested in the lottery?"

Don Camillo blushed. "You have misunderstood me," he protested. "When I said 'someone' I hadn't the faintest intention of alluding to You! I was speaking in a general sense."

"I am glad of that, Don Camillo," said the Lord with grave approval. "It is very wise, when discussing such matters, always to speak in a general sense."

A few days later Don Camillo received a summons to the villa of the Signora Carolina, the lady of Boscaccio, and when he came home he was fairly bursting with joy. "Lord!" exclaimed Don Camillo, halting breathlessly before the altar. "To-morrow You will see before You a lighted candle of twenty pounds' weight. I am going now to the town to buy it, and if they haven't got one I shall have it specially made."

"But, Don Camillo, where will you get the money?"

"Don't You worry, Lord. You shall have Your candle if I have to sell the mattress off my bed to pay for it! Look what You have done for me!" Then Don Camillo calmed down a little. "The Signora Carolina is giving an offering to the church of all the money needful for casting a new Geltrude!"

"And how did she come to think of it?"

"She said she had made a vow," explained Don Camillo, "to the effect that if the Lord helped her to bring off a certain business deal she would give a bell to the church. Thanks to Your intervention, the deal was successful, and within a month's time Geltrude will once more lift up her voice to heaven! I am going now to order the candle!"

The Lord checked Don Camillo just as he was making off under full steam.

"No candles, Don Camillo," said the Lord severely. "No candles."

"But why?" demanded Don Camillo in amazement.

"Because I do not deserve them," replied the Lord. "I have given the Signora Carolina no help of any kind in her affairs. I take no interest in competition or in commerce. If I were to intervene in such matters the winner would have reason to bless Me, while the loser would have cause to curse Me. If you happen to find a purse of money, I have not made you find it, because I did not cause your neighbour to lose it. You had better light your candle in front of the middleman who helped the Signora Carolina to make a profit of nine million. I am not Myself a middleman."

The Lord's voice was unusually severe and Don Camillo was filled with shame.

"Forgive me," he stammered. "I am a poor, obtuse, ignorant country priest and my brain is filled with fog and foolishness."

The Lord smiled. "Don't be unjust to Don Camillo," He exclaimed. "Don Camillo always understands Me, and that is clear proof that his brain is not filled with fog. Very often it is precisely the intellect that fogs the brain. It is not you who have sinned; indeed, your gratitude touches Me because in any small matter that gives you pleasure you are always ready to perceive the kindness of God. And your joy is always honest and simple, as it is now in the thought of once more having your bell. And as it is also in your desire to thank Me for having enabled you to have it. But the Signora Carolina is neither simple nor honest when she sets out to acquire money by enlisting God's help in her shady financial transactions."

Don Camillo had listened silently and with his head bowed. Then he looked up. "I thank You, Lord. And now I shall go and tell that usurer that she can keep her money! My bells must all be honest bells. Otherwise it would be better to die without ever again hearing Geltrude's voice!"

He wheeled round, proud and determined, and the Lord smiled as He watched him walk away. But as Don Camillo reached the door, the Lord called him back.

"Don Camillo," said the Lord, "I am perfectly aware of all that your bell means to you, because I can always read your mind at any moment, and your renunciation is so fine and noble that in itself alone it would suffice to purify the bronze of a statue of Antichrist. *Vade retro, Satana!* Get out of here quickly or you will compel Me to grant you not only your bell, but who knows what other development."

Don Camillo stood quite still. "Does that mean I can have it?"

"It does. You have earned it."

In such contingencies Don Camillo invariably lost his head. As he was standing before the altar he bowed, spun on his heel, set off at a run, pulled himself up half-way down the nave and finally skidded as far as the church door. The Lord looked on with satisfaction, because even such antics may at given moments be a manner of praising God.

And then a few days later there occurred an unpleasant incident. Don Camillo surprised an urchin busily engaged in adorning the newly whitened walls of the presbytery with a piece of charcoal and saw red. The urchin made off like a lizard, but Don Camillo was beyond himself and gave chase.

"I shall collar you if I burst my lungs!" he yelled.

He set off on an infuriated pursuit across the fields and at every step his ire increased. Then suddenly the boy, finding his escape blocked by a thick hedge, stopped, threw up his arms to shield his head and stood still, too breathless to utter a word.

Don Camillo bore down on him like a tank and, grasping the child's arm with his left hand, raised the other, intending dire punishment. But his fingers closed on an arm so slender and emaciated that he let go and both his own arms fell to his sides. Then he looked more attentively at the boy and found himself confronted by the white face and terrified eyes of Straziami's son.

Straziami was the most unfortunate of all Peppone's faithful satellites, and this not because he was an idler: he was in fact always in search of a job. The trouble lay in the fact that, having secured one, he would stick to it quietly for one day and on the second he would have a row with his employer, so that he seldom worked more than five days a month.

"Don Camillo," the child implored him, "I'll never do it again!"

"Get along with you," said Don Camillo abruptly.

Then he sent for Straziami, and Straziami strode

defiantly into the presbytery with his hands in his pockets and his hat on the back of his head. "And what does the people's priest want with me?" he demanded arrogantly.

"First of all that you take off your hat or else I knock it off for you; and, secondly, that you stop hectoring, because I won't put up with it."

Straziami himself was as thin and as colourless as his son and a blow from Don Camillo would have felled him to the ground. He threw his hat on to a chair with an elaborate assumption of boredom.

"I suppose you want to tell me that my son has been defacing the Archbishop's Palace? I know it already; someone else told me. Your grey Eminence need not worry: this evening the boy shall have his hiding."

"If you dare so much as to lay a finger on him I'll break every bone in your body," shouted Don Camillo. "Suppose you give him something to eat! Haven't you realized that the wretched child is nothing but a skeleton?"

"We aren't all of us the pets of the Eternal Father," began Straziami sarcastically.

But Don Camillo interrupted him: "When you

do get a job, try to keep it instead of getting thrown out on the second day for spouting revolution!''

"You look after your own bloody business!" retorted Straziami furiously. He turned on his heel to go, and it was then that Don Camillo caught him by the arm. But that arm, as his fingers grasped it, was as wasted as that of the boy and Don Camillo let go of it hastily.

Then he went off to the Lord above the altar. "Lord," he exclaimed, "must I always find myself taking hold of a bag of bones?"

"All things are possible in a country ravaged by so many wars and so much hatred," replied the Lord with a heavy sigh. "Suppose you tried keeping your hands to yourself?"

Don Camillo went next to Peppone's workshop and found him busy at his vice.

"As mayor it is your duty to do something for that unhappy child, Straziami's," said Don Camillo.

"With the funds available to the commune, I might possibly be able to fan him with the calendar on that wall," replied Peppone.

"Then do something as chief of your beastly

Party. If I am not mistaken, Straziami is one of your star scoundrels."

"I can fan him with the blotter from my desk."

"Heavens above! And what about all the money they send you from Russia?"

Peppone worked away with his file. "The Red Tsar's mails have been delayed," he remarked. "Why can't you lend me some of the cash you get from America?"

Don Camillo shrugged his shoulders. "If you can't see the point as mayor or as Party leader, I should have thought you might understand as the father of a son (whoever may be his mother!) the need for helping that miserable child who comes and scribbles on the presbytery wall. And by the way, you can tell Bigio that unless he cleans my wall free of charge I shall attack your Party from the Demo-Christian news-board."

Peppone carried on with his filing for a bit; then he said: "Straziami's boy isn't the only one in the commune who needs to go to the sea or to the mountains. If I could have found the money I should have established a colony long ago."

"Then go and look for it!" exclaimed Don Camillo. "So long as you stay in this office and file bolts, mayor or no mayor, you won't get hold of money. The peasants are stuffed with it."

"And they won't part with a cent, *reverendo*. They'd shell out fast enough if we suggested founding a colony to fatten their calves! Why don't you go yourself to the Pope or to Truman?"

They quarrelled for two hours and very nearly came to blows at least thirty times. Don Camillo was very late in returning to the presbytery.

"What has happened?" asked the Lord. "You seem upset."

"Naturally," replied Don Camillo. "When an unhappy priest has had to argue for two hours with a Communist mayor in order to make him understand the necessity for founding a seaside colony, and for another two hours with a miserly woman capitalist to get her to fork out the money required for that same colony, he may justly feel a bit gloomy."

"I understand you," replied the Lord.

Don Camillo hesitated. "Lord," he said at last, "You must forgive me if I have dragged even You into this business of the money."

"Me?"

"Yes, Lord. In order to compel that usurer to

part with her cash, I had to tell her that I saw You in a dream last night and that You told me You would rather her money went for a work of charity than for the buying of the new bell."

"Don Camillo! And after that you have the courage to look Me in the eyes?"

"Yes," replied Don Camillo calmly. "The end justifies the means."

"Machiavelli doesn't strike Me as being one of those sacred scriptures upon which you should base your actions," exclaimed the Lord.

"Lord," replied Don Camillo, "it may be blasphemy to say so, but even he can sometimes have his uses."

"And that is true enough," agreed the Lord.

Ten days later, when a procession of singing children passed by the church on their way to the colony, Don Camillo hurried out to say good-bye and to bestow stacks of little holy pictures. And when he came to Straziami's boy at the end of the procession he frowned at him fiercely. "Wait until you are fat and strong and then we shall have our reckoning!" he threatened.

Then, seeing Straziami, who was following the children at a little distance, he made a gesture of disgust. "Family of scoundrels," he muttered as he turned his back and went into the church.

That night he dreamed that the Lord appeared to him and said that He would sooner the Signora Carolina's money were used for charity than for the purchase of a bell.

"It is already done," murmured Don Camillo in his sleep.

FEAR

Peppone finished reading the newspaper that
had come by the afternoon post and then spoke
to Smilzo, who was awaiting orders perched on a
high stool in a corner of the workshop.

"Go and get the car and bring it here with the
squadron in an hour's time."

"Anything serious?"

"Hurry up!" shouted Peppone.

Smilzo started up the lorry and was off, and
within three-quarters of an hour he was back again
with the twenty-five men of the squadron. Peppone climbed in and they were very soon at the
People's Palace.

"You stay here and guard the car," Peppone

ordered Smilzo, "and if you see anything odd, shout."

When they reached the assembly room Peppone made his report. "Look here," he said, thumping with his big fist upon the news-sheet, which bore enormous headlines, "matters have reached a climax: we are for it. The reactionaries have broken loose, our comrades are being shot at and bombs are being thrown against all the Party headquarters."

He read aloud a few passages from the paper, which was in point of fact the *Milano Sera*, a Milanese evening publication. "And note that we are told these things not by one of our Party papers! This is an independent newspaper and it is telling the truth, because you can read it all clearly printed under the headlines!"

"Just think of it!" growled Brusco. "If one of those independent papers that always favour the right so damnably and oppose us whenever they can, is compelled to publish such things, only think how much worse the reality must be! I can't wait to read to-morrow's *Unità*!"

Bigio shrugged his shoulders . "It'll probably be tamer than this," he said. "*Unità* is run by comrades who are active, but all of them educated persons of culture who are learned in philosophy, and they always tend to minimize such matters, so as to avoid exciting the people."

"Yes; educated folk who are careful to observe rules and to do nothing illegal," added Pellerossa.

"More like poets than anything else!" concluded Peppone. "But all the same they are people who, once they do pick up a pen, strike so hard that they would knock out the Eternal Father!"

They continued to discuss the situation, reading over again the principal statements in the Milanese paper and commenting upon what they had read.

"It is obvious that the Fascist revolution has already begun," said Peppone. "At any moment, here where we stand, we may expect the flying squads to burn the Co-operatives and the people's houses and beat folk up and purge them. This paper mentions 'Fascist cells' and 'storm-troopers'; there is nothing equivocal about it. If it were a case of simple *qualunquismo*,* capitalism or monar-

* Italian party entitled "L'Uomo Qualunque": equivalent to "The Man in the Street".

chism they would speak of reactionaries, of 'nostal-gists,' etcetera. But here they put it perfectly clearly and bluntly as 'fascism' and 'flying squads'. And bear in mind that it's an independent paper. We must be ready to face up to any eventuality."

Lungo gave it as his opinion that they ought to move first before the others got going: they knew perfectly well every individual reactionary in the commune. "We should go to every house in turn and pull them out and beat them up, and we should do it without any further talk."

"No," Brusco objected. "It seems to me that we should be putting ourselves in the wrong from the start. Even this paper says that we should reply to provocation, but not invite it. Because if we give provocation we give them the right to retaliate."

Peppone agreed. "If we are to beat up anybody we should do it with justice and democratically."

They went on talking more quietly for another hour and were suddenly roused by an explosion that shook the windows. They all rushed out of the building and found Smilzo lying full length behind the lorry, as though he were dead, with his face covered with blood. They handed over the unconscious man to his wife's care and leaped into the lorry.

"Forward!" bawled Peppone as Lungo bent to the wheel.

Off went the lorry at full tilt, and it was not until they had covered a couple of miles that Lungo turned to Peppone.

"Where are we going?"

"That's just it," muttered Peppone. "Where are we going?"

They stopped the car and collected themselves. Then they turned round and went back to the village and drew up in front of the Demo-Christian headquarters. There they found a table, two chairs and a picture of the Pope, and all these they threw out of the window. Then they climbed into the lorry again and set out firmly for Ortaglia.

"Nobody but that skunk Pizzi would have thrown the bomb that killed Smilzo," said Peller-ossa. "He swore vengeance on us that time when we quarrelled over the labourers' strike. 'We shall see!' he said."

They surrounded the house, which was isolated, and Peppone went in. Pizzi was in the kitchen stirring the *polenta*. His wife was laying the table and his little boy was putting wood on the fire.

Pizzi looked up, saw Peppone and immediately realized that something was wrong. He looked at the child, who was now playing on the floor at his feet. Then he looked up again.

"What do you want?" he asked.

"They have thrown a bomb in front of our headquarters and killed Smilzo!" shouted Peppone.

"Nothing to do with me," replied Pizzi.

The woman caught hold of the child and drew back.

"You said that you would make us pay dearly when we came up against you over the labourers' strike. You are a reactionary swine, anyway."

Peppone bore down on him menacingly, but Pizzi stepped back a pace and, catching up a revolver that lay on the mantelpiece, he pointed it at Peppone. "Hands up, Peppone, or I shoot you!"

At that moment somebody who was hiding outside threw open the window, fired a shot and Pizzi fell to the ground. As he fell his revolver went off and the bullet lost itself among the ashes on the hearth. The woman looked down at her husband's body and put her hand in front of her mouth. The child flung himself on his father and began screaming.

Peppone and his men climbed hastily into the lorry and went off in silence. Before reaching the village they stopped, got out and proceeded separately on foot.

There was a crowd in front of the People's Palace, and Peppone met Don Camillo coming out of it.

"Is he dead?" Peppone asked.

"It would take a lot more than that to kill a fellow of his stamp," replied Don Camillo, chuckling. "Nice fool you've made of yourself destroying the table at the Demo-Christian headquarters. They won't half laugh at you!"

Peppone looked at him gloomily. "There isn't much to laugh at, when people begin throwing bombs."

Don Camillo looked at him with interest. "Peppone," he said. "One of two things: either you are a scoundrel or a fool."

In point of fact, Peppone was neither. He quite simply did not know that the explosion had not been caused by a bomb, but by one of the retreaded tyres of the lorry, from which a piece of rubber had struck the unfortunate Smilzo in the face.

He went to look underneath the lorry and saw the disembowelled tyre and then thought of Pizzi lying stretched out on the kitchen floor, of the woman who had put her hand to her mouth to stifle her screams and of the screaming child.

And meanwhile people were laughing. But within an hour the laughter died down because a rumour had spread through the village that Pizzi had been wounded.

He died next morning, and when the police went to question his wife the woman stared at them with eyes that were blank with terror.

"Didn't you see anyone?"

"I was in the other room; I heard a shot and ran in and found my husband lying on the ground. I saw nothing else."

"Where was the boy?"

"He was already in bed."

"And where is he now?"

"I've sent him to his grandmother."

Nothing more could be learned. The revolver was found to have one empty chamber, the bullet that had killed Pizzi had hit him in the temple and its calibre was identical with that of those remaining in the revolver. The authorities promptly decided that it was a case of suicide.

Don Camillo read the report and the statements made by various persons to the effect that Pizzi had been worried for some time past by the failure of an important deal in seeds, and had been heard to say on several occasions that he would like to make an end of it all. Then Don Camillo went to discuss the matter with the Lord.

"Lord," he said unhappily, "this is the first time in my parish that someone has died to whom I cannot give Christian burial. And that is right enough, I know, because he who kills himself kills one of God's children and loses his soul, and, if we are to be severe, should not even lie in consecrated ground."

"That is so, Don Camillo."

"And if we decide to allow him a place in the cemetery, then he must go there alone, like a dog, because he who renounces his humanity lowers himself to the rank of a beast."

"Very sad, Don Camillo, but so it is."

The following morning (it happened to be a Sunday) Don Camillo, in the course of his Mass, preached a terrible sermon on suicide. It was pitiless, terrifying and implacable.

"I would not approach the body of a suicide," he said in his peroration, "not even if I knew that my doing so would restore him to life!"

Pizzi's funeral took place on that same afternoon. The coffin was pushed into a plain third-class hearse which set out jerkily, followed by the dead man's wife and child and his two brothers in a couple of two-wheeled carts. When the convoy entered the village people closed their shutters and peeped through the cracks.

Then suddenly something happened that struck everybody speechless. Don Camillo unexpectedly made his appearance, with two acolytes and the cross, took up his station in front of the hearse and preceded it on foot, intoning the customary psalms.

On reaching the church square, Don Camillo beckoned to Pizzi's two brothers, and they lifted the coffin from the hearse and carried it into the church, and there Don Camillo said the office for the dead and blessed the body. Then he returned to his position in front of the hearse and went right through the village, singing. Not a soul was to be seen.

At the cemetery, as soon as the coffin had been lowered into the grave, Don Camillo drew a deep breath and cried in a stentorian voice: "May God reward the soul of His faithful servant, Antonio Pizzi."

Then he threw a handful of earth into the grave, blessed it and left the cemetery, walking slowly through the village depopulated by fear.

"Lord," said Don Camillo when he reached the church, "have You any fault to find with me?"

"Yes, Don Camillo, I have: when one goes to accompany a poor dead man to the cemetery one should not carry a pistol in one's pocket."

"I understand, Lord," replied Don Camillo. "You mean that I should have kept it in my sleeve so as to be more accessible."

"No, Don Camillo, such things should be left at home, even if one is escorting the body of a . . . suicide."

"Lord," said Don Camillo after a long pause,

"will You have a bet with me that a commission composed of my most assiduous bigots will write an indignant letter to the bishop, to the effect that I have committed a sacrilege in accompanying the body of a suicide to the cemetery?"

"No," replied the Lord. "I won't bet, because they are already writing it."

"And by what I have done I have drawn upon myself the hatred of everyone: of those who killed Pizzi, of those who, while well aware, like everybody else, that Pizzi had been murdered, found it inconvenient that doubts should be raised regarding his suicide. Even of Pizzi's own relations, who would have been glad to have it believed that there was no suspicion that he had not killed himself. One of his brothers asked me: 'But isn't it forbidden to bring a suicide into the church?' Even Pizzi's own wife must hate me, because she is afraid, not for herself, but for her son, and is lying in order to defend his life."

The little side door of the church creaked and Don Camillo looked round as Pizzi's small son entered. The boy came forward and halted in front of Don Camillo.

"I thank you on behalf of my father," he said in

the grave, hard voice of a fully grown man. Then he went away as silent as a shadow.

"There," said the Lord, "goes someone who does not hate you, Don Camillo."

"But his heart is filled with hatred of those who killed his father, and that is another link in an accursed chain that no one succeeds in breaking. Not even You, who allowed Yourself to be crucified for these mad dogs."

"The end of the world is not yet," replied the Lord serenely. "It has only just begun, and up There time is measured by millions of centuries. You must not lose your faith, Don Camillo. There is still any amount of time."

THE FEAR CONTINUES

AFTER THE publication of his parish magazine, Don Camillo found himself quite alone.

"I feel as though I were in the middle of a desert," he confided to the Lord. "And it makes no difference even when there are a hundred people around me, because although they are all there, within half a yard of me, there seems to be a thick wall of glass that divides us. I hear their voices, but as though they came from another world."

"It is fear," replied the Lord. "They are afraid of you."

"Of me!"

"Of you, Don Camillo. And they hate you.

They were living warmly and comfortably in their cocoon of cowardice. They were perfectly aware of the truth, but nobody could compel them to recognize it, because nobody had proclaimed it publicly. You have acted and spoken in such a manner that they are now forced to face up to it, and it is for that reason that they hate and fear you. You see your brothers who, like sheep, are obeying the orders of a tyrant and you cry: 'Wake up out of your lethargy and look at those who are free; compare your lives with those of people who enjoy liberty!' And they will not be grateful to you but will hate you, and if they can they will kill you, because you compel them to face up to what they already knew but for love of a quiet life pretended not to know. They have eyes, but they will not see. They have ears, but they will not hear. You have given publicity to an injustice and have placed these people in a serious dilemma: if you hold your tongue you condone their imposition; if you don't condone it you must speak out. It was so much easier to ignore it. Does all this surprise you?"

Don Camillo spread out his arms. "No," he said. "But it would have surprised me had I not known that You were crucified for telling people the truth. As it is, it merely distresses me."

Presently there came a messenger from the bishop. "Don Camillo," he explained, "Monsignore has read your parish magazine and is aware of the reactions it has aroused in the parish. The first number has pleased him, but he is exceedingly anxious that the second number shouldn't contain your obituary. You must see to it."

"That matter is independent of the will of the publishers," replied Don Camillo, "and therefore any request of the kind should be addressed not to me, but to God."

"That is exactly what Monsignore is doing," explained the messenger, "and he wished you to know it."

The sergeant of police was a man of the world: he met Don Camillo by chance in the street. "I have read your magazine, and the point you make about the tyre tracks in the Pizzis' yard is very interesting."

"Did you make a note of them?"

"No," replied the sergeant. "I didn't make a note of them because directly I saw them I had casts taken of them then and there, and happened to discover, quite by chance, when I was comparing the casts with the wheels of various local cars, that those tracks had been made by the mayor's lorry. Moreover, I observed that Pizzi had shot himself in the left temple when he was holding the revolver in his right hand. And when I hunted among the ashes in the fireplace I found the bullet that left Pizzi's revolver when Pizzi fell, after the other bullet had been fired at him through the window.''

Don Camillo looked at him sternly. "And why have you not reported all this?"

"I have reported it in the proper quarter, *reverendo*. And I was told that if, at such a moment, the mayor was arrested the matter would immediately assume a political significance. When such things get mixed up with politics there are complications. It is necessary to wait for an opportunity, and you, Don Camillo, have supplied it. I have no wish to shift my responsibility on to other shoulders; I merely want to avoid the danger that the whole business should get bogged because there are people who wish to make a political issue of it."

Don Camillo replied that the sergeant had acted most correctly.

"But I can't detail two constables to guard your back, Don Camillo."

"It would be a blackguardly attack!"

"I know it; but all the same I would surround you with a battalion if it were in my power," muttered the sergeant.

"It isn't necessary, sergeant. Almighty God will see to it."

"Let's hope He'll be more careful than He was of Pizzi," the sergeant retorted.

The following day the inquiries were resumed and a number of landowners and leaseholders were interrogated. As Verola, who was among those questioned, protested indignantly, the sergeant replied very calmly:

"My good sir: given the fact that Pizzi had no political views and that nobody robbed him of anything, and given also the fact that certain new evidence tends to suggest a murder rather than a suicide, we must exclude the supposition that we are dealing with either a political crime or a robbery. We must therefore direct our inquiries towards those with whom Pizzi had business or friendly relations and who may have borne him a grudge."

The matter proceeded in this manner for several days and the persons questioned were furiously angry.

Brusco also was infuriated, but he held his tongue.

"Peppone," he said at last, "that devil is playing with us as though we were kids. You'll see. When he has questioned everybody he can think of, including the midwife, in a couple of weeks' time he'll be coming to you with a smile to ask whether you have any objection to his questioning one of our people. And you won't be able to refuse, and he will begin his questioning and out will come the whole business."

"Don't be ridiculous," shouted Peppone. "Not even if they tore out my nails."

"It won't be you they'll question, or me, or the others we are thinking of. They'll go straight for the one who will spill everything. They'll tackle the man who fired the shot."

Peppone sniggered. "Don't talk rubbish! When we ourselves don't know who did it!"

And thus it was. Nobody had seen which of the twenty-five men of the squadron had done the deed. As soon as Pizzi had fallen they had all of them climbed into the lorry and later on had separated without exchanging a single word. Since then nobody had even mentioned the matter.

Peppone looked Brusco straight in the eyes. "Who was it?" he asked.

"Who knows? It may have been you yourself."

"I?" cried Peppone. "And how could I do it when I wasn't even armed?"

"You went alone into Pizzi's house and none of us could see what you did there."

"But the shot was fired from outside, through the window. Someone must know who was stationed at that window."

"At night all cats are grey. Even if someone did see, by now he has seen nothing at all. But one person did see the face of the man who fired, and that was the boy. Otherwise his people wouldn't have said that he was in bed. And if the boy knows it then Don Camillo also knows it. If he hadn't known he wouldn't have said or done what he has said and done."

"May those who brought him here roast in Hell!" bawled Peppone.

Meanwhile, the net was being drawn closer and closer, and every evening, as a matter of discipline, the sergeant went off to inform the mayor of the progress of the inquiries.

"I can't tell you more at the moment, Mr. Mayor," he said one evening, "but we know where we are at last; it seems that there was a woman in the case."

Peppone merely replied, "Indeed!" but he would gladly have throttled him.

It was already late in the evening and Don Camillo was finding jobs for himself in the empty church. He had set up a pair of steps on the top step of the altar, for he had discovered a crack in the grain of the wood of one arm of the crucifix and having filled it up was now applying a little brown paint to the white plaster of the stopping.

At a certain moment he sighed and the Lord spoke to him in an undertone. "Don Camillo, what is the matter? You haven't been yourself for several days past. Are you feeling unwell? Is it perhaps a touch of influenza?"

"No, Lord," Don Camillo confessed without raising his head. "It is fear."

"You are afraid? But of what, in Heaven's name?"

"I don't know. If I knew what I was afraid of I shouldn't be frightened," replied Don Camillo. "There is something wrong, something in the air, something against which I can't defend myself. If twenty men came at me with guns I shouldn't be afraid. I should only be angry because they were twenty and I was alone and had no gun. If I found myself in the sea and didn't know how to swim I'd think: 'There now, in a few moments I shall drown like a kitten!' and that would annoy me very much but I should not be afraid. When one understands a danger one isn't frightened. But fear comes with dangers that are felt but not understood. It is like walking with one's eyes bandaged on an unknown road. And it's a beastly feeling."

"Have you lost your faith in your God, Don Camillo?"

"*Da mihi animam, caetera tolle.* The soul is of God, but the body is of the earth. Faith is a great thing, but this is a purely physical fear. I may have immense faith, but if I remain for ten days without drinking I shall be thirsty. Faith consists in enduring that thirst in serenity as a trial sent by God. Lord, I am willing to suffer a thousand fears such as this one for love of You. But nevertheless I am afraid."

The Lord smiled.

"Do You despise me?"

"No, Don Camillo; if you were not afraid, what value would there be in your courage?"

Don Camillo continued to apply his paint-brush carefully to the wood of the crucifix and his eyes were fixed upon the Lord's hand, pierced by the nail. Suddenly it appeared to him that this hand came to life, and at exactly that moment a shot resounded through the church.

Somebody had fired through the window of the little side chapel.

A dog barked, and then another; from far away came the brief burst of a tommy-gun firing. Then there was silence once more. Don Camillo gazed with scared eyes into the Lord's face.

"Lord," he said, "I felt Your hand upon my forehead."

"You are dreaming, Don Camillo."

Don Camillo lowered his eyes and fixed them upon the hand pierced by the nail. Then he gasped and the brush and the little pot of paint fell from his fingers.

The bullet had passed through the Lord's wrist.

"Lord," he said breathlessly, "You pushed back my head and Your arm received the bullet that was meant for me!"

"Don Camillo!"

"The bullet is not in the wood of the crucifix!" cried Don Camillo. "Look where it went!"

High up to the right and opposite the side chapel hung a small frame containing a silver heart. The bullet had broken the glass and had lodged itself exactly in the centre of the heart.

Don Camillo ran to the sacristy and fetched a long ladder. He stretched a piece of string from the hole made by the bullet in the window to the hole made in the silver heart. The line of the string passed at a distance of about twelve inches from the nail in the Lord's hand.

"My head was just there," said Don Camillo, "and Your arm was struck because You pushed my head backwards. Here is the proof!"

"Don Camillo, don't get so excited!"

But Don Camillo was beyond recovering his composure, and had he not promptly developed a fierce temperature the Lord only knew what he might have done. And the Lord obviously did know it, because He sent him a fever that laid him low in his bed as weak as a half-drowned kitten.

The window through which the shot had been fired gave on to the little enclosed plot of land that belonged to the church, and the police sergeant and Don Camillo stood there examining the church wall.

"Here is the proof," said the sergeant, pointing to four holes that were clearly visible upon the light distemper just below the window-sill. He took a penknife from his pocket, dug into one of the holes and presently pulled out some object.

"In my opinion, the whole business is quite simple," he explained. "The man was standing at some distance away and fired a round with his tommy-gun at the lighted window. Four bullets struck the wall and the fifth hit the glass and went through it."

Don Camillo shook his head. "I told you that it was a pistol shot and fired at close range. I am not yet so senile as to be unable to distinguish a pistol shot from a round of machine-gun fire! The pistol shot came first and was fired from where we are standing. Then came the burst from the tommy-gun from further away."

"Then we ought to find the cartridge-case near-by," retorted the sergeant; "and it isn't anywhere to be seen!"

Don Camillo shrugged his shoulders. "You would need a musical critic from La Scala to distinguish by the key tone whether a shot comes from an automatic or from a revolver! And if the fellow fired from a pistol he took the cartridge-case with him."

The sergeant began to nose around, and presently he found what he was looking for on the trunk of one of the cherry trees that had been planted in a row some five or six paces from the church.

"One of the bullets has cut the bark," he said. And it was obvious that he was right. He scratched his head thoughtfully. "Well," he said, "we may as well play the scientific detective!"

He fetched a pole and stuck it into the ground close to the church wall, in front of one of the bullet holes. Then he began to walk to and fro with his eyes fixed on the damaged cherry tree, moving to right or left until the trunk was in a direct line covering the pole by the wall. Thus he ultimately found himself standing in front of the hedge, and beyond the hedge were a ditch and a lane.

Don Camillo joined him and, one on either side of the hedge, they carefully examined the ground. They went on searching for a while, and after about five minutes Don Camillo said: "Here it is," and held up a tommy-gun cartridge-case. Then they found the other three.

"That proves I was right," exclaimed the sergeant. "The fellow fired from here through the window."

Don Camillo shook his head. "I've never used a tommy-gun," he said, "but I know that with other guns bullets never describe a curve. See for yourself."

Just then a constable came up to inform the sergeant that everyone in the village was quite calm.

"Many thanks!" remarked Don Camillo. "Nobody fired at any of them! It was me that they shot at!"

The sergeant borrowed the constable's rifle and lying flat on the ground aimed in the direction of the upper pane of the chapel window where, so far as his memory served him, he thought the bullet had struck it.

"If you fired now, where would the bullet go?" asked Don Camillo.

It was an easy reckoning, mere child's play: a bullet fired from where they were and passing through the chapel window would have hit the door of the first confessional on the right-hand side, at about three yards' distance from the church door.

"Unless it was a trained bullet, it couldn't have gone past the altar, not if it split itself!" said the sergeant. "Which only goes to show," he went on, "that any matter in which you are mixed up is always enough to make one tear out one's hair! You couldn't be contented with one assailant! No, sir: you must have two of them. One that fires from behind the window and another that fires from behind a hedge a hundred and fifty paces away."

"Oh well, that's how I'm made," replied Don Camillo. "I never spare expense!"

That same evening Peppone summoned his staff and all the local Party officials to head-quarters.

Peppone was gloomy. "Comrades," he said, "a new event has occurred to complicate the present situation. Last night some unknown person shot at the so-called parish priest and the reaction is taking advantage of this episode in order to raise its head and throw mud at the Party. The reaction, cowardly as always, has not the courage to speak out openly, but, as we would expect, is whispering in corners and trying to saddle us with the responsibility for this attack."

Lungo held up his hand and Peppone signed to him that he could speak.

"First of all," said Lungo, "we might tell the reactionaries that they had better offer proof that there really has been an attempt on the priest's life. Since there seem to have been no witnesses, it might easily be that the reverend gentleman himself fired off a revolver in order to be able to attack us in his filthy periodical! Let us first of all obtain proof!"

"Excellent!" exclaimed his audience. "Lungo is perfectly right!"

Peppone intervened. "One moment! What Lungo says is fair enough, but we should not exclude the possibility that what we have heard is the truth. Familiar as we all are with Don Camillo's character, it can hardly be said, honestly, that he is in the habit of using underhand methods . . ."

Peppone was in his turn interrupted by Spocchia, the leader of the cell at Milanetto. "Comrade Peppone, do not forget that once a priest always a priest! You are letting yourself be carried away by sentimentality. Had you listened to me, his filthy magazine would never have seen the light and to-day the Party would not have had to endure all the odious insinuations with regard to Pizzi's suicide! There should be no mercy for the enemies of the people! Anyone who has mercy on the people's enemies betrays the people!"

Peppone crashed his fist down on the table. "I don't require any preaching from you!" he bawled.

Spocchia seemed unimpressed. "And, moreover, if instead of opposing us you had let us act while there was still time," he shouted, "we shouldn't now be held up by a crowd of accursed reactionaries! I . . ."

Spocchia was a thin young man of twenty-five and sported an immense head of hair. He wore it brushed back, waved on top of his head and smooth at the sides, forming a kind of upstanding crest such as is affected by louts in the north and by the boors of Trastevere. He had small eyes and thin lips.

Peppone strode up to him aggressively. "You are a half-wit!" he said, glaring at him.

The other changed colour, but made no reply.

Returning to the table, Peppone went on speaking. "Taking advantage of an episode that is based only upon the statement of a priest," he said, "the reaction is putting forward fresh speculations to the discredit of the people. The comrades need to be more than ever determined. To such ignoble suggestions they . . ."

Quite suddenly something happened to Peppone that had never happened to him before: Peppone began *listening to himself*. It seemed to him as though Peppone were among his audience listening to what Peppone was saying:

". . . *and their bodies sold, the reaction paid by the enemies of the proletariat, the labourers starved . . .*" Peppone listened and gradually he seemed to be listening to another man. ". . . *the Savoy gang . . . the lying clergy . . . the black government . . . America . . . plutocracy . . .*"

"What in the world does plutocracy mean? Why

is that fellow spouting about it when he doesn't even know what it means?" Peppone was thinking. He looked round him and saw faces that he barely recognized. Shifty eyes, and the most treacherous of all were those of young Spocchia. He thought of the faithful Brusco and looked for him, but Brusco stood at the far end of the room, with folded arms and bent head.

"But let our enemies learn that in us the Resistance has not weakened. . . . The weapons that we took up for the defence of liberty . . ." And now Peppone heard himself yelling like a lunatic, and then the applause brought him back to himself.

"Splendid!" whispered Spocchia in his ear as they went downstairs. "You know, Peppone, it only needs a whistle to set them going. My lads could be ready in an hour's time."

"Good! Excellent!" replied Peppone, slapping him on the shoulder. But he would gladly have knocked him down. Nor did he know why.

He remained alone with Brusco and at first they were silent.

"Well!" exclaimed Peppone at last. "Have you lost your wits? You haven't even told me whether I spoke well or not?"

"You spoke splendidly," replied Brusco, "wonderfully. Better than ever before." Then the curtain of silence fell back heavily between them.

Peppone was doing accounts in a ledger. Suddenly he picked up a glass paper-weight and threw it violently on to the ground, bellowing a long, intricate and infuriated blasphemy. Brusco stared at him.

"I made a blot," explained Peppone, closing the ledger.

"Another of that old thief Barchini's pens," remarked Brusco, being careful not to point out to Peppone that, as he was writing in pencil, the explanation of the blot did not hold water.

When they left the building and went out into the night they walked together as far as the cross-roads and there Peppone pulled up as though he had something that he wished to tell Brusco. But he merely said: "Well; see you to-morrow."

"To-morrow then, Chief. Good night."

"Good night, Brusco."

MEN OF GOODWILL

CHRISTMAS WAS approaching, and it was high time to get the figures of the Crib out of their drawer so that they might be cleaned, touched up here and there and any stains carefully removed. It was already late, but Don Camillo was still at work in the presbytery. He heard a knocking on the window and on seeing that it was Peppone went to open the door.

Peppone sat down while Don Camillo resumed his work and neither of them spoke for quite a long time.

"Hell and damnation!" exclaimed Peppone suddenly and furiously.

"Couldn't you find a better place to blaspheme

in than my presbytery?" inquired Don Camillo
quietly. "Couldn't you have got it off your chest at
your own headquarters?"

"One can't even swear there any longer," muttered Peppone. "Because if one does someone asks
for an explanation."

Don Camillo applied a little white lead to St.
Joseph's beard.

"No decent man can live in this filthy world!"
exclaimed Peppone after a pause.

"How does that concern you?" inquired Don
Camillo. "Have you by any chance become a decent
man?"

"I've never been anything else."

"There now! And I should never have thought
it." Don Camillo continued his retouching of St.
Joseph's beard. Then he began to tidy up the
saint's clothing.

"How long will you be over that job?" asked
Peppone angrily.

"If you were to give me a hand, it would soon be
done."

Peppone was a mechanic and he possessed hands
as big as shovels and enormous fingers that gave an
impression of clumsiness. Nevertheless, when any-

body wanted a watch repaired, they never failed to take it to Peppone. Because it is a fact that it is precisely such bulky men that are best adapted to the handling of minute things. Peppone could streamline the body of a car or the spokes of a wheel like a master painter.

"Are you crazy! Can you see me touching up saints!" he muttered. "You haven't by any chance mistaken me for a sacristan?"

Don Camillo fished in the bottom of the open drawer and brought forth a pink-and-white object about the size of a sparrow: it was in fact the Holy Infant Himself.

Peppone hardly knew how he came to find it in his hands, but he took up a little brush and began working carefully. He and Don Camillo sat on either side of the table, unable to see each other's faces because of the light of the lamp between them.

"It's a beastly world," said Peppone. "If you have something to say you daren't trust anyone. I don't even trust myself."

Don Camillo appeared to be absorbed in his task: the Madonna's whole face required repainting. "Do you trust me?" he asked casually.

"I don't know."

"Try telling me something and then you will know."

Peppone completed the repainting of the Baby's eyes, which were the most difficult part. Then he touched up the red of the tiny lips. "I should like to give it all up," said Peppone, "but it can't be done."

"What prevents you?"

"Prevents me? With an iron bar in my hand, I could stand up to a regiment!"

"Are you afraid?"

"I've never been afraid in my life!"

"I have, Peppone. Sometimes I am frightened."

Peppone dipped his brush in the paint. "Well, so am I, sometimes," he said, and his voice was almost inaudible.

Don Camillo sighed. "The bullet was within four inches of my forehead," said Don Camillo. "If I hadn't drawn my head back at that exact moment I should have been done for. It was a miracle."

Peppone had completed the Baby's face and was now working with pink paint on His body.

"I'm sorry I missed," he mumbled, "but I was too far off and the cherry trees were in the way."

Don Camillo's brush ceased to move.

"Brusco had been keeping watch for three nights round the Pizzi house to protect the boy. The boy must have seen who it was that fired at his father through the window, and whoever did it knows that. Meanwhile I was watching your house. Because I was certain that the murderer must know that you also knew who killed Pizzi."

"The murderer: who is he?"

"I don't know," replied Peppone. "I saw him from a distance creeping up to the chapel window. But I wasn't in time to fire before he did. As soon as he had fired I shot at him and I missed."

"Thank God," said Don Camillo. "I know how you shoot, and we may say that there were two miracles."

"Who can it be? Only you and the boy can tell."

Don Camillo spoke slowly. "Yes, Peppone, I do know; but nothing in this world could make me break the secrecy of the confessional."

Peppone sighed and continued his painting.

"There is something wrong," he said suddenly. "They all look at me with different eyes now. All of them, even Brusco."

"And Brusco is thinking the same thing as you

are, and so are the rest of them," replied Don Camillo. "Each of them is afraid of the others and every time any one of them speaks he feels as if he must defend himself."

"But why?"

"Shall we leave politics out of it, Peppone?"

Peppone sighed again. "I feel as if I were in gaol," he said gloomily.

"There is always a way out of every gaol in this world," replied Don Camillo. "Gaols can only confine the body, and the body matters so little."

The Baby was now finished and it seemed as if His clear, bright colouring shone in Peppone's huge dark hands. Peppone looked at Him and he seemed to feel in his palms the living warmth of that little body. He forgot all about being in gaol.

He laid the Baby delicately upon the table and Don Camillo placed the Madonna near Him.

"My son is learning a poem for Christmas," Peppone announced proudly. "Every evening I hear his mother teaching it to him before he goes to sleep. He's a wonder!"

"I know," agreed Don Camillo. "Look how beautifully he recited the poem for the bishop!"

Peppone stiffened. "That was one of the most

rascally things you ever did!" he exclaimed. "I shall get even with you yet."

"There is plenty of time for getting even, or for dying," Don Camillo replied.

Then he took the figure of the ass and set it down close to the Madonna as she bent over her Child. "That is Peppone's son, and that is Peppone's wife, and this one is Peppone," said Don Camillo, laying his finger on the figure of the ass.

"And this one is Don Camillo!" exclaimed Peppone, seizing the figure of the ox and adding it to the group.

"Oh well! Animals always understand one another," said Don Camillo.

And though Peppone said nothing he was now perfectly happy, because he still felt in the palm of his hand the living warmth of the pink Baby; and for a time the two men sat in the dim light looking at the little group of figures on the table and listening to the silence that had settled over the Little World of Don Camillo, and that silence no longer seemed ominous but instead full of peace.